Rekindled Faith

A heartwarming story of hope, empathy, and be resilience of friendship

By

Philip DeLizio

This is a work of fiction. Names, characters, places, and incidents either are the product of the author's imagination or are used fictitiously. Any resemblance to actual persons, living or dead, events, or locales is entirely coincidental.

Copyright © 2024 by Philip DeLizio

All rights reserved. No part of this book may be reproduced or used in any manner without written permission of the copyright owner except for the use of quotations in a book review. For more information, delizio1722@comcast.net

First paperback edition June 2024

ISBN: Printed in the United States

www.delizioauthor.com

Published by Hemingway Publishers

Cover design by Hemingway Publishers

ABOUT THE AUTHOR

Dr. Philip DeLizio, Ed. D. is a retired school teacher. Upon his retirement, he began to write inspirational books for teens and young adults based on his experiences in the classroom, hoping his words would be inspirational and uplifting to his readers.

Books

Teen/Young Adult Inspirational Books

Rekindled Faith

Emma's Dilemma

A Light on the Horizon

Darkness to Light

A Letter of Hope

Crossroads

Paul Phillips Mysteries

Twisted Reckonings

Shadows in the Jungle

The Missing Piece

The Cricketeer's Conspiracy

Shadows of the Past

DEDICATION

Dedicated to my niece Savanah.

I love you.

In "Rekindled Faith" by Philip DeLizio, two 14-year-old girls from different backgrounds, Olivia and Janice, form an unlikely friendship. Olivia, from an affluent family, struggles to connect with her faith despite her privileged life. Janice, who has faced immense hardship after losing her parents, finds solace in her strong faith and works to support her grandmother. As their friendship blossoms, they face opposition from their peers and families, testing the strength of their bond. Through misunderstandings, personal crises, and societal pressures, Olivia and Janice must navigate their differences while staying true to their friendship. Their journey leads them to a deeper understanding of their faith and the power of forging true connections in the face of adversity. "Rekindled Faith" is a heartwarming story of hope, empathy, and the resilience of friendship, offering a powerful message about the impact of love, compassion, and forgiveness in overcoming societal divisions.

Table Of Contents

ABOUT THE AUTHOR 3

DEDICATION 5

CHAPTER 1 A CHANCE ENCOUNTER 8

CHAPTER 2 BUDDING FRIENDSHIP 23

CHAPTER 3 WHISPERS AND RUMORS 35

CHAPTER 4 STRENGTH IN ADVERSITY 48

CHAPTER 5 SEEKING ANSWERS 60

CHAPTER 6 CHALLENGE FROM WITHIN 71

CHAPTER 7 CHALLENGE FROM WITHOUT 82

CHAPTER 8 TOUCHING LIVES 92

CHAPTER 9 FALLING OUT 103

CHAPTER 10 HEALING BEGINS 113

CHAPTER 11 COMING TOGETHER 124

CHAPTER 12 LIGHT IN DARK TIMES 136

CHAPTER 13 GROWTH AND GRATITUDE 148

CHAPTER 14 FAREWELLS AND HELLOS 162

CHAPTER 15 A FUTURE OF PROMISE 178

CHAPTER 1
A CHANCE ENCOUNTER

A Sunday Morning at Church

The sun shone through the windows of the Westside Community Church, casting beams of light across the wooden pews. Hymns of praise echo off the high ceiling as the congregation sings in acapella, harmonious union. There is a warm and welcoming atmosphere, with pews arranged in neat rows facing the altar. The altar itself is adorned with flowers and candles, creating a peaceful and sacred space.

This is a place that encourages reflection and reverence. Olivia sat between her parents, tugging at the fancy dress her mother had picked out. She always found the sermons a bit dull, even if the message of faith and goodness was important. Gazing up, she wonders what Jesus would say to make faith feel truly alive. As the service neared its close, Olivia fidgeted with the hem of her skirt. She spies her little brother playing with toy figurines near the aisle and stifles a giggle.

14-year-old Olivia Hanson has long brown hair and green eyes. She is of average height and build for her age. She usually dresses in modest, stylish clothes and sometimes wears a small cross necklace. She comes from an affluent family and lives in a nice neighborhood. Her parents are both successful professionals. She has one sibling, a younger brother named Ethan. They are a close-knit family that spends a lot of time together. They attend church every Sunday, as her parents have always emphasized the importance of faith in their lives.

Growing up had been an interesting journey for Olivia. She has always been the curious kind, always questioning things around her and seeking deeper meaning. Her parents always encouraged her intellectual pursuits and education, so she has had many opportunities to learn and grow. However, despite the privileges she has had, she struggled to find a deeper connection with her faith. Attending church every Sunday with her family has been a constant, but she has often felt like something is amiss. She has been on a quest to understand and explore her faith more deeply and to find that sense of connection for which she longs.

The Hansons live in a charming suburban neighborhood in the town of Meadowville. The streets are lined with well-kept houses, and there are plenty of trees and gardens that add to the beauty of the area. It is a close-knit community where people often know and support one another.

Olivia knows most of her neighbors. There are a few who even stand out to her. The Smiths, an older couple who have lived next door for as long as she can remember. They are incredibly kind and always ready to lend a helping hand. They have a beautiful garden that they take great pride in. Sometimes, Olivia will stop by just to admire their flowers and have a chat.

Another favorite neighbor is Mrs. Jenkins, a retired teacher who lives across the street. She is a wise and compassionate woman, always willing to share her knowledge and experiences. Olivia will often find herself seeking her advice when faced with difficult decisions or needing guidance. She feels these neighbors have truly enriched the community with their warmth and kindness. They make living there feel like being part of an extended family. It is quite comforting to know that they can rely on one another, and Olivia is grateful for their presence in her life.

The Hanson home is quite spacious and comfortable. When you first walk in, there is a cozy foyer with a small table where keys and such are kept. The walls are painted a warm cream color, and there is a soft carpet beneath your feet. On the left is a cozy living room with plush sofas and bookshelves filled with all sorts of novels, Bibles, and philosophical texts.

Adjacent to the living room is the dining area, with a large wooden table where the family gathers for meals. The room is adorned with artwork and a display cabinet filled with precious family heirlooms. Beyond the dining area is our kitchen, with sleek countertops and modern appliances.

Upstairs, you will find the bedrooms. Olivia's room is her sanctuary for reflection and meditation. It is lined with soft lighting and a desk where she writes and ponders life's big questions. Ethan's room is filled with his favorite toys and posters. The Hansons' bedroom is elegant and serene, with a comfortable bed and a view of the garden outside.

Olivia has always been empathetic towards others and has a strong desire to help those in need. It is something that has been instilled in her by her parents from a young age. She finds fulfillment in volunteering and making a positive impact in her community. Growing up in Meadowville has been a journey of self-discovery, questioning, and seeking ways to connect more deeply with her faith and make a difference in the world. And she has achieved a bit on all the things, but one, and that is "connecting more deeply with her faith."

As church services were coming to a close, Janice was rushing down the sidewalk a few blocks away, panting as she dashed toward the church. She glances fretfully at her watch and curses under her breath at the late hour. Her grandmother had already left for the morning service, unwilling to be held back by Janice's poor timekeeping.

The previous night, Janice had worked a double shift at the diner owned by her grandmother's friend, which was how she was able to work at the age of 14 just to earn some extra cash. Exhaustion dragged on her weary body, but she knew rest would have to wait. Sunday service with her grandma was non-negotiable.

Janice Thompson is a resilient and spiritual kid whose background has been shaped by some tough experiences. She lost her parents at an early age in a traffic accident, which was an incredibly difficult time for her. It plunged her into the foster care system, which was a challenging and uncertain time in her life. But thankfully, Janice's grandmother fought to adopt her and has since become her rock.

She lives in a small neighborhood, tucked away in a peaceful corner of town, away from the 'nice' houses where Olivia lives. Although it may not be the most glamorous or bustling neighborhood, it is a place that feels like home to Janice as it is comforting and offers a safe environment. Her neighborhood is close to a small park with a playground where children can be seen playing and laughing on sunny afternoons.

Within walking distance to Janice's house is a small grocery store and a few independently owned businesses that serve the community. The Westside Community Church is within walking distance, too, but walking there takes a while.

Janice's home is cozy and filled with love. It is not noticeably big, but it is her safe haven. There is a small living room where she spends most of her good time with her grandmother and a simple kitchen where her grandmother prepares delicious meals. Janice's bedroom is her little sanctuary, filled with books and a desk where she reads and writes whenever she can. The Thompsons may not have much but they happily make the most of what they do have. Home truly is where the heart is, and Janice is profoundly grateful for the warmth and love that fills her humble space.

Janice is African American, pretty, and of average height with a slender build. She has curly black hair that she usually ties up in a messy bun. Her warm brown eyes often reflect deep thoughtfulness. She has a scar above her left eyebrow from a childhood fall, which she wears proudly. If you ask her, she will say she has a simple and natural look, nothing extraordinary. She has come to embrace her looks as a part of who she is.

Losing her parents at such an early age taught Janice the value of cherishing the time we have with our loved ones. It also made her grow up faster and take on more responsibilities to help support her grandmother financially. It has not always been easy, but Janice says it has made her a stronger person. Being in foster care taught her the importance of empathy and compassion. She saw firsthand the struggles that many other kids faced. It motivated her to give back and help others and her grandmother has shown her what it means to be selfless and to love unconditionally.

All these experiences have played a significant role in shaping who Janice is today. They have taught her resilience, empathy, and the importance of having faith in both her and in something or someone greater than she was. Life has thrown its fair share of challenges her way, but she tries her best to view them as opportunities for growth and learning. Janice believes that everything happens for a reason, even if it is difficult to understand at that moment. Sure, there have been times when she felt frustrated or overwhelmed by circumstances, but she has learned to channel those emotions into fuel for personal growth. Forced to grow up quicker than a child would want, she has chosen to focus on the positives in her life, like the love and support of her grandmother and the friendships she formed along the way.

Being bitter does not serve any purpose, Janice has learned, and it only weighs you down. Instead, she chooses to have faith and trust in the belief that life has a way of working itself out. While she has faced many challenges, she tries to approach them with resilience and a hopeful mindset, letting go of bitterness and embracing the opportunities for growth that they provide.

As the church building came into view, Janice pushed her tired legs to move faster. Her now-unbound hair blew wildly in the wind, strands sticking to her damp cheeks. The plain dress chosen from haste bore wrinkles and stains from her labor. As she entered the church, the large oak doors burst open with a bang, drawing everyone's eyes. Janice rushed inside, brows furrowed in panic, only to find the service was almost over. Her windblown hair was disheveled, and she struggled to catch her breath. She hurried down the aisle, eyes scanning frantically for her grandmother's familiar face.

In her haste, she was not watching where she was going and crashed right into Olivia, who had turned to see the commotion. Olivia's hot chocolate splashed all over as the cup tumbled to the floor. Horror filled Janice's eyes at the mess she had caused with her lateness. But even though she was disheveled and out of sorts, kindness remained her guide.

"I am so sorry!" the girl gasped, mortified. She hurried to gather napkins from her bag to soak up the spill. Olivia sat stunned, hot chocolate staining her white dress and soaking in swiftly until she noticed the girl trying in vain to clean the mess alone. After the initial shock wore off, she took in Janice's disheveled attire and panicked expression.

"It's okay, accidents happen," she said gently. With a small smile, she decided to help, finding more wisdom in kindness over judgment. Janice's eyes glistened, unused to such easy forgiveness.

"Please, let me help clean up. It's the least I can do." She insisted.

Olivia accepted, sensing a good soul beneath the frantic surface. As they set to work mopping the mess, there was a friendly exchange of words, and a tentative bond began to form. Flustered, Janice grabbed several napkins, hurriedly dabbing at the stain spreading across Olivia's dress.

"I am so sorry!" she repeated, wiping in vain at the soaked fabric.

Olivia placed a hand on Janice's restless one. "Thank you, but it was an accident. Don't trouble yourself."

17

Janice shook her head. "Please, it makes me feel better."

Her smile held no trace of pretense, only guileless care. Olivia smiled back gently. "Then I appreciate your help. And do not worry, it will wash out."

A blossom of understanding took root, hints of an unlikely bond prompting hopes for friendship where there seemed little chance. Kneeling to clean the floor, Janice whispered as she worked. "My name is Janice. Sorry again for the mess."

"It's alright, my name is Olivia." Her dress was ruined, but curiosity lingered about this stranger. "Crazy morning?"

Janice sighed. "Overslept after a late shift. God, I hope Gram is not upset with me!" She said with a visible frown and genuine worry.

Olivia glimpsed a woman beyond her frazzled facade, clearly responsible beyond her youth. "What do you do?" she asked politely.

"I work at a diner. Gotta help Gram somehow," Janice replied matter-of-factly.

Though drained, her smile remained tender. Despite differences in dress and demeanor, a spark of kinship kindled between them. Olivia observed in Janice a strength of spirit, whereas others may see only exhaustion. And in Olivia's gentle manner, Janice sensed a caring wish to understand. Their contrasting lives held more that united than divided them.

With the mess now cleaned, more remained to learn through blossoming the fellowship. As they wiped, Janice told Olivia of her work routine and Olivia shared about school. A rapport blossomed between them through open dialogue.

Noticing a glint, Olivia smiled. "I like your necklace. Is that a charm?"

Janice's fingers traced its shape fondly. "Yeah, my mom gave it to me before…" Her tone dimmed.

Olivia touched her arm gently. "I am sure she would be proud of the woman you are becoming."

Welling in tears, Janice smiled. "Thanks...you are sweet. I could sit with you next Sunday. If your parents do not mind."

Olivia beamed. "I would like that."

She sensed in Janice a kindred soul worth knowing beyond this chance meeting. Their stark differences seemed to complement rather than divide them. From hardship, Janice blossomed with compassion, and in her light, Olivia felt that faith dwells as much in the lives we touch as it does in the scriptures. Beyond the mess lay the seeds of an unexpected friendship, and both sensed in it solace to nurture life's beauty. The last napkin was deposited in the trash. The spill was cleaned but something new had begun between the girls through this not-very-planned meeting.

As the final song was coming to an end, Olivia's gaze strayed to the front row, where Janice sat engaged but peaceful. Her presence added mystery to faith and its people. It prodded Olivia to see and question beyond what meets the eye. She wondered why she had never noticed Janice before today. And something told her this day would remain remembered for its glimpses into life's surprises and the connections capable of transforming two solitary souls who assumingly came from two very different lives.

For now, the sermon's lessons seemed newly illuminated through one chance encounter and the understanding sown through simple kindness.

Olivia replayed the pastor's words in her mind: "Kindness is the quality of being friendly, generous, and considerate. It comes in many forms and may not always be as simple as doing good things. What comes as "good" and "right" for someone may not necessarily be viewed as such by another. Different people tend to look at kindness in different ways. But empathy, understanding, and compassion are universal. Accepting and helping everyone, no matter who they are or where they came from, is kindness in and of itself. Kindness is one of the attributes of God and one of the components of the fruit of the Spirit. Therefore, Christians are expected to express kindness in their daily conversations."

Catching Janice's eye, Olivia offered a parting smile. "Thank you for everything. See you around?"

Janice's returning grin shimmered with promise. "For sure." She made her exit, her gait now lighter as she sought out her grandmother carefully in the lined crowd.

Olivia watched her go, tracing the shapes of Janice's worn dress and tangled hair. Beyond surface differences hinted understanding, and a spark of curiosity stirred for the journey of her new friend's heart and mind.

Thus, through happenstance, a bond between seekers of truth was allowed to take root where, before, just two kindred spirits were walking alone on two separate roads. In that moment of chance and the insight it awoken, Olivia and Janice glimpsed destiny may arrive, both quiet and unexpected, and meeting by circumstance proved but the first step toward a friendship destined to impact their journey in faith and life.

CHAPTER 2
BUDDING FRIENDSHIP

Olivia sat in her regular pew at Westside Community Church. This seemed like the longest week of her life as she anxiously waited for Sunday. Glancing around more eagerly than usual for any sign of Janice. Last Sunday's chance encounter played in her mind; how Janice's act of kindness in helping clean up the spill transformed a potentially awkward situation into the genesis of an unexpected connection.

The week between their first meeting and today was quite eventful for Olivia. After their initial conversation, she could not stop thinking about Janice and the genuine connection they had formed. During that week, she found herself questioning her own faith even more. Janice's unwavering devotion and strong faith despite her hardships intrigued and confused Olivia at the same time. She wondered if there was something she was missing or perhaps

23

if there was a deeper meaning to her own faith that she had not fully explored.

She spent quite a bit of time reading and reflecting, trying to make sense of it all. She delved into books on spirituality, philosophy, and, of course, the Bible to gain a broader perspective. She found this verse that stuck with her: Proverbs 16:9, "In their hearts, humans plan their course, but the Lord establishes their steps." Olivia pondered this for a while. Even though a meeting may seem like a chance to us, it is possible that God had a purpose in bringing people together. It was an introspective week for her, filled with deep contemplation and a search for answers. She also could not help but wonder how Janice was doing. She knew she had her own struggles, and Olivia hoped she was okay. She wanted to see her again, to continue their conversations and learn from her experiences.

As the service began, Olivia spotted a familiar face slip into the back row. Janice gave a small wave and smile, which Olivia returned with a warm grin. She was surprised at how happy it made her to see Janice again. Throughout the sermon, Olivia found herself distracted, flitting her gaze over to her new friend, curious what paths their budding relationship may forge. Janice met her glance occasionally and seemed equally curious about continuing their talk after the service ended.

For Janice, she felt the same excitement as Olivia, waiting for Sunday to come around. She could not stop thinking about their conversation either. It was refreshing to connect with someone so different yet so genuine. Janice could not deny the doubts creeping in. She wondered if their differences would eventually drive them apart or if their friendship could withstand the judgments of others. Sometimes, Janice questioned if she was enough and if her past and her circumstances made her unworthy of a friendship with someone like Olivia. But despite those insecurities, she could not deny the growing connection she felt with Olivia.

When the final hymn concluded, Janice waited by the heavy oak doors for Olivia. As Olivia approached, she said, "I'm glad you came," and meant it.

"Me too. This past week felt longer, knowing I would see you again today."

For both girls, it was as if everything fell back into place. Their conversations flowed effortlessly, and they realized that their bond felt stronger than any doubts or judgments. Together, they exited into the sunny morning, ready to journey along pathways of faith and fellowship as unlikely friends discovering shared truths.

Finding an empty bench outside the church, the girls sat down. Olivia grinned. "So, what have you been up to?" Janice told her about her shifts at the diner, working hard to help her grandmother.

"But enough about that. What about you? How was school?" Olivia shared some highlights from her classes and mentioned a new book club she thought Janice might enjoy. As they talked, both girls realized how happy it made them to spend this time with someone who truly listened without judgment.

Olivia and Janice go to different schools. Olivia attends an expensive private school known for its academic excellence. It is quite different from Janice's public school, as Olivia's has a more affluent student population and offers a wide range of extracurricular activities. She also has access to advanced resources and facilities to support her learning.

Janice, on the other hand, attends a public school with fewer resources and a more diverse student body. However, they both share a love for learning and are equally eager to pursue their education.

A comfortable silence fell as they sat lost in thought. But the smiles on their young faces showed their pleasure in this emerging friendship and hope for nurturing its growth in the weeks and fellowship to come. Olivia found her attention drawn not to looking for her family but to her new friend, wondering what unseen wellspring nourished Janice's devout spirit through life's difficulties. While her own faith sometimes felt surface-level, Janice embodied a deep well of conviction. Even through sorrows, she possessed a gift Olivia admired: finding light where others saw shadow. Olivia sensed divinity resonated more truly in Janice's being, and she envied possessing such resilient roots of belief Janice had planted within.

Her trials fortified her faith rather than weakened it. Olivia marveled that despite hardship, Janice maintained gardens of grace where blessings could bloom. In that moment, catching a faint smile playing on Janice's lips uplifted by some profound message, Olivia wished for the wellspring sustaining her friend to nourish her own spirit also. As the congregation continued to file out of the church, Olivia and Janice lingered on the bench.

"I was thinking about what you said last week," Janice began hesitantly. "About losing my mom and dad. It is still hard sometimes." Olivia took her hand in a gesture of comfort. "I cannot imagine how difficult that must have been. You are so strong."

Janice shook her head. "I don't feel strong. Just trying to keep going for grandma."

Olivia related how she admired Janice's devotion yet still grappled with deeper questions. "My faith feels superficial. When you believe so truly, what gives you that strength?" Squeezing Olivia's hand,

Janice said simply, "Love. I know they are with God, watching over me. And knowing other people struggle too, that helps me believe we are not alone." Her wisdom resonated with Olivia, who felt their friendship had only begun revealing life's profound mysteries.

Olivia smiled at Janice. "You know, on the surface, our lives seem so different. But talking with you, I feel like we understand each other."

Janice nodded. "I was thinking that too. We both want the same things: to honor our families, have a purpose, and find our way. Maybe the paths are different, but the destinations could be the same."

"And it helps to have someone by your side on the journey," Olivia added. An understanding passed between them of lives that, at face value, diverged vastly but, in spirit, contained mirrored hopes. Behind walls, erecting divisions in society lay the common ground of souls seeking meaning.

In each other they glimpsed reflections neither saw in those around them. Kinship was kindling between them, unlike souls who surprisingly spoke the same language of compassion. Their chatter flowed on, pruning prejudices to uncover fertile soil where friendship might take root and bloom unexpectedly yet all the richer for overcoming distances.

Olivia's parents and brother were leaving the church at the same time as Janice's grandmother. They said their goodbyes until next time and went their separate ways.

After arriving home, Olivia replayed her afternoon with Janice. At dinner, Olivia shared with her family, "I met someone; her name is Janice," Olivia said eagerly.

Her parents exchanged glances. "Janice...?" her father questioned. "She seems nice but comes from a harder background," her mother said delicately. "Just be careful, darling. You come from different worlds." Olivia felt stung.

"You do not know her. She is wonderful, kind, and faithful."

"We don't doubt her goodness. Only wonder if she understands the expectations of our community." Her father took her hand. "Guard your heart, sweet pea. Some folks may not understand."

Olivia's parents are, as Olivia describes them, wonderful individuals who have always supported her and fostered her growth. Sarah and Michael Hanson. Sarah works as a lawyer, and Michael is a business executive. They are loving and caring and always prioritize spending time as a family. They encourage their children to pursue their interests and explore different avenues of learning.

30

Olivia's brother Ethan is a few years younger than her. They share a close bond despite their difference in age. Ethan is a smart and energetic kid, always eager to learn new things. Olivia and Ethan spend a lot of time together, whether it is playing games, helping each other with homework, or just hanging out as siblings do. Olivia is truly grateful to have such a supportive and loving family. They have played a significant role in shaping who she is and instilling important values in her life.

Though annoyed with her parents about what they said about Janice, Olivia did not show concern. She believed good existed beyond what some perceived as "different." Her friendship with Janice had only begun, and she vowed to nurture what she knew in her soul was true. That evening, Olivia tried to shrug off her parents' comments, yet could not help feeling restless. What if others disapproved, too? Still, she recalled Janice's smile and knew there lay mysteries begging discovery unlike any sermon could offer.

As she readied for bed that evening, Olivia glimpsed her reflection and wondered what Janice saw in her from beyond those perceived worlds apart. Determination swelled to understand this unique soul and nurture what truths might bloom from the soil where none expected. If Janice could find her place, Olivia vowed to make one for her in a community she hoped preached compassion, not division.

With evening's quiet, doubts receded while likings flourished anew. Intrigue overcame apprehension, drawing Olivia towards Janice in spirit, though far apart, curious to glimpse the world from her unique vantage. Slumber came with anticipation of next Sunday's fellowship and what wonders may unfold.

Janice bustled about the kitchen, helping her grandmother prepare dinner. "You will never guess who I met, Gran," she said excitedly. As Janice recounted meeting Olivia, her grandmother listened with a smile. But she also knew life's cruelties.

"I am glad you have found a friend, dear. However, her world is much different than ours. Are you sure you will not get hurt?"

Janice paused, understanding her gram's concern. "Olivia's kind. I think if we give each other a chance, our differences will not matter."

Her grandmother squeezed her hand. "I hope you are right, child. Just take care of that big heart of yours."

Though uncertainty lingered in her grandmother's words, Janice believed her bond with Olivia could overcome any divide. As they sat down to eat, she said a silent prayer that her new friend would offer joy to balance life's hardships. That night, as Janice lay in bed gazing at patterns moonlight traced on her ceiling, she thought of Olivia and felt grateful for their friendship taking root. Though life remained hard, Olivia's kindness lit her path, reminding Janice she was not alone.

As she does every night, not knowing Olivia has the same ritual, Janice recited her favorite Bible verse, Jeremiah 29:11. "For I know the plans I have for you," declares the Lord, "plans to prosper you and not to harm you, plans to give you hope and a future." It is a reminder that even during challenges, God has a purpose and plan for our lives.

Meanwhile, at her home, Olivia peered out her window at starlit skies and wondered what worlds Janice saw looking upwards from her bed. Their lives seemed so different yet talking with Janice filled emptier parts of Olivia in ways church failed to. Where before she felt detached, now purpose stirred for nurturing the bond kindled between them and sharing life's beauty despite sorrows.

Olivia started thinking about the many verses in the Bible she loved to read over and over. There were so many beautiful verses in the Bible that she felt spoke to her in diverse ways. One that has always resonated with her is Philippians 4:13: "I can do all things through Christ who strengthens me." It reminded Olivia that she is never alone and that with God's strength, she can overcome any challenge or obstacle that comes her way. It is a verse that gives her hope and reassurance in times of doubt or uncertainty.

As sleep descended, each girl smiled at the mysteries the day had unfolded: how, in a chance meeting, spilled hot chocolate paved pathways leading them to one another's lives. Their budding friendship proved joy could emerge when least expected, in the most unlikely of places, if hearts embraced empathy over fear. And in quiet moments before dreams took hold, each sent thanks heavenward for this gift of compassion beginning to heal solitary souls.

CHAPTER 3
WHISPERS AND RUMORS

The next Sunday, Olivia and Janice walked into Westside Community Church, laughing together about something funny that had happened at school during the week. Olivia's teacher, Mr. Jenkins, was trying to explain ancient Egyptian hieroglyphics. But instead of drawing a graceful bird, he accidentally drew something that looked like a potato with wings! Even though they did not go to the same school, they still managed to find ways to share funny moments and make each other laugh. Janice thought it was a cool part of their friendship.

Too immersed in their cheerful conversation, they did not initially notice the disapproving looks and murmurs coming from some of the regular parishioners. "Can you believe Mrs. Peterson gave me detention for forgetting my science homework?" asked Janice, still chuckling at the memory. "As if I do not have enough to do already!"

Olivia grinned. "At least it is not for the rest of the semester like my teacher threatened me with last month. Teachers have no tolerance for teenage antics."

They made their way to the second pew, chatting happily. But then Janice caught a phrase from sisters Betty and Martha, seated in front of them. "Those girls, spending so much time together...it is just not right."

Betty and Martha, they are quite the duo! Betty, the elder sister, is 16 years old, and Martha is 12. Betty is an outgoing and spirited person. She has a contagious energy that lights up any room she enters. She is a natural leader and is always organizing activities and events for her friends and classmates. Betty loves adventure and is always up for trying new things.

On the other hand, Martha is a bit more reserved and introspective. She is a deep thinker and loves spending her time reading and writing. Martha has a quiet strength about her and is incredibly empathetic. She can pick up on other people's emotions and is always there to support and listen to others when they need it. Despite their different personalities, Betty and Martha have an incredibly close bond. They balance each other out and make a great team.

Betty encourages Martha to step out of her comfort zone and try new things, while Martha provides a calming presence and offers thoughtful advice to Betty. They are always there for each other through thick and thin, and their sisterly love is truly inspiring to witness.

Janice nudged Olivia and nodded subtly toward the sisters. Olivia's smile faded as she overheard more murmurs from other corners of the church. "Such different backgrounds can only lead to trouble." "Her parents must be so ashamed, cavorting with that charity case."

Olivia was taken aback when Betty and Martha expressed their concern about her spending time with Janice. Olivia knew the sisters very well, or so she thought. They were considered friends, never having a cross word between them. However, Olivia sort of understood where they were coming from. They care about Olivia and want what is best for her. But it did catch Olivia off guard because she did not expect them to see it that way. She guessed they perceived her friendship with Janice as a bit unconventional due to their different backgrounds and social circles. Perhaps they worry that Janice's struggles and hardships could somehow have a negative impact on her.

37

But Olivia knew that Janice had been such a positive influence in her life. Janice has shown Olivia a different perspective and has deepened her understanding of faith and compassion. Olivia knows they have a genuine connection, and their friendship has been a source of support and personal growth for both. Olivia hoped that, over time, Betty and Martha would come to see the value and strength in Olivia's friendship with Janice.

Hurt flooded Janice's chest, but she took a calming breath. Getting angry would not help the situation. But she wondered sadly how long it would be before these callous whispers reached her grandmother's ears and put doubts in her mind about the friendship. For now, she focused on being there for Olivia, whose questioning gaze showed she had also heard the unkind remarks. Janice gave her friend's hand a comforting squeeze under the pew, and Olivia managed a small, grateful smile in return.

Olivia continued to notice Betty and Martha craning their necks to sneak glances at her and Janice. She strained her ears to listen as they murmured to each other.

"Such a shame that Janice has attached herself to Olivia. That poor girl does not know what is good for her."

Olivia felt indignant but stayed silent, not wishing to cause a scene. "With her background, she will only serve to drag Olivia down from her high place in society," Martha whispered disapprovingly.

Olivia clenched her fists, anger building inside her. How dare they make such harmful assumptions? Janice's character had nothing to do with her past; she was one of the kindest, most caring people Olivia knew. As the sermon began, Olivia tried to push aside the hurtful words and focus on the message. But she could not help shooting angry looks at Betty and Martha's turned backs. Their close-minded gossip had succeeded only in strengthening Olivia's resolve to stand by her friend no matter what.

What an ironic situation. Betty and Martha talk badly about Janice, while at the same time, the Pastor speaks about the importance of not judging others based on their backgrounds or circumstances but rather showing empathy and understanding. The sermon emphasized the need to extend a helping hand to those in need, even if they may be different from us. It was a powerful message, and it resonated with Olivia deeply, considering the judgment Janice was facing from some people in the community.

Janice excused herself to use the bathroom. As she pushed open the ladies' room door, she heard giggling from within.

"I mean, can you believe Janice thinks she can hang out with Olivia?" said a haughty voice. Janice recognized the voice as belonging to Claire, a snobbish girl in Olivia's class. Claire is quite the character. She is always dressed in the latest designer clothes and seems to have this air of superiority about her. The kind of person who thinks they are better than everyone else. She has that perfect posture and that smug smile that can really get under your skin. She is also quick to judge others based on their appearance or social status. It is like she is always looking for ways to make herself feel superior.

Another voice, this one unrecognized by Janice, "I know, who does she think she is? Like someone from her background could ever be accepted by Olivia's fancy family."

Stunned, Janice froze in the doorway. She had not thought people would be so cruel. What had she ever done to these girls to deserve their jealousy and scorn? Just then, Claire turned and caught sight of Janice. A guilty flush crept

40

up her cheeks at being overheard. But she quickly recovered her sneer.

"Well...are you just going to stand there listening to our private conversation?" Claire snapped, crossing her arms confrontationally. Hurt and embarrassed, Janice backed away without a word. As she rushed back to her seat, tears stung her eyes. She could not understand why others refused to see her humanity. When the service ended, Olivia and Janice walked out together silently.

Olivia could sense Janice's distress under her brave smile. "Janice...are you okay?" Olivia asked hesitantly. Janice took a shaky breath. She did not want to tell Olivia about Claire. She did not want to burden her with unnecessary drama or create tension between them. Janice was also struggling with her own self-doubts, questioning if she could handle the situation on her own. It was a tough decision, but she thought it would be better to handle it herself and protect Olivia from the negativity. Janice did what she thought was best at the time.

"Of course," Janice replied, mustering her brightest smile despite its fragility. "Why would I not be ok?" Olivia saw through Janice's brave act but did not push her further.

She simply slipped her hand into Janice's and gave it a gentle, understanding squeeze.

Janice's smile became a little more genuine then. She was grateful beyond words for Olivia's compassion and support. It gave her strength to believe in their friendship despite the prejudice trying to undermine it. Hand in hand, they walked out into the sunny day, both vowing silently to stay true to this bond that was helping heal their lonely souls.

Another week went by. The girls seldom see each other during the week, so they need routines to keep them busy. Even though they do not see each other much, Janice and Olivia try to stay connected. They often text or call each other to check in, share updates, and have meaningful conversations. It is important to them to maintain their friendship and support each other, even when they are apart. They share thoughts, dreams, and sometimes even their struggles. It helps them feel connected and reminds them of the bond they have.

Janice's weekly routine is to work part-time at the diner on Saturdays and occasionally a weeknight or two, which helps support her grandmother financially. On weekdays, she focuses on her studies and spends time with my grandmother, making sure she is doing okay. Janice also enjoys volunteering at a local soup kitchen and reading books that promote personal growth. This helps her stay connected to her faith and find comfort in helping others.

Not surprisingly, Olivia's weekly routines are not unlike those of Janice's. During the week when she does not see Janice, Olivia usually focuses on her schoolwork and spends time with her family. She also enjoys reading, writing, and volunteering at the local library. She will sometimes take long walks around the neighborhood to reflect on things. It is important for her to stay engaged and to keep exploring her faith, so she will often read the Bible and have discussions with her parents about different spiritual ideas.

Sunday finally arrived, and both girls were overly excited and rushed to Church. As the service began, Olivia and Janice found it difficult to focus. Each was lost in turmoil inside her own mind. Now that they were together, Olivia began to doubt whether she should really care what Betty, Martha, or anyone else thought. Janice had proven to be a true friend; was that not what really mattered? Meanwhile, Janice felt a cold knot of shame harden in her stomach. She knew some came from wealthier families, so was she really worthy of being Olivia's friend? What if Claire was right? What if she truly did not belong?

Staring blankly at the pastor, neither girl heard a word of his sermon. Their minds swam with insecurity and self-doubt sown by the cruel, judgmental whispers against their blossoming friendship. Glancing at each other, Olivia and Janice saw mirrored in each other's eyes the pain and confusion caused by prejudices not of their own making. Silently, they pledged to face these trials together and to stay true to the bond that gave both girls a sense of belonging.

After the service, Olivia's parents approached her with another gentle word of caution about Janice. Olivia bit her tongue, tired of defending her friend. Janice chatted with Olivia's brother, Ethan, making him laugh despite her somber mood. But then she glanced up and met the icy stare of Martha across the courtyard. Martha looked Janice up and down with blatant pity and disapproval as if seeing something unclean. Janice recoiled inwardly from that stare, which seemed to dig into her deepest insecurities and made her want to run away in tears.

She forced a smile at Ethan and bid a hasty goodbye, discreetly dabbing at her eyes. Her own grandmother's critical gaze sometimes hurt her, too, she could not bear it from strangers as well. Janice's heart grew heavy at the prospect of such sneers following her everywhere. But thoughts of Olivia waiting for her outside lifted her feet, determined to keep faith in the one soul who looked past the surface and accepted her for who she was.

That evening, as Olivia lay in bed thinking, doubts crept in. Were Betty and Martha, right? Were their differences too great? She and Janice came from such different worlds. But when they were together, everything felt so simple and true.

Across town, Janice tossed and turned as fear kept her awake. Clara's harsh words re-played in her head. Did she truly have a place in Olivia's bright, polished circles? Janice knew how hard her grandmother worked to give her stability; what if clinging to their friendship only caused trouble?

With a sigh, Olivia resolved to push aside the fears for now. Janice had become her closest confidante, her best friend, a beacon of strength. Their bond was more than surface judgments allowed.

Rolling onto her side, Janice remembered Olivia's patience and smile that day. Beyond opinions or backgrounds, they simply enjoyed each other's company. That was enough for now. Doubt could not sever the tightening threads that stitched their solitary souls together into one tapestry of friendship.

Both girls finally drifted to sleep, comforted that though trials may come, their bond was a sheltering place where each found belonging.

The next morning, as Olivia and Janice went about their daily routines, unease still lingered in both their minds. Could gossip and prejudice really fracture what they had found in each other? Janice wondered as she helped her grandmother with chores. Their union felt so pure and true; surely hatred could not destroy it. Olivia recalled Betty and Martha's scornful glares, and doubt needled her. What if disapproval chipped away at Janice's confidence until their friendship cracked? She did not know if she was strong enough to defy everyone.

That evening, Janice sat kneading bread dough for hours, lost in worries. Olivia lay awake staring at the dark ceiling, similarly tormented. Both girls were exhausted yet could not find rest. But somewhere deep within, a stubborn flame still burned, a flame kindled by their chance meeting, now fueled by the true understanding that transcended surface differences. Both girls turned to their Bibles for solace and answers. They believe it is important to focus on the love and compassion they have for each other rather than letting doubts or outside opinions cloud their relationship.

They both want to approach the situation with an open heart and seek guidance from God to understand the meaning of friendship and how it can transcend social boundaries. Janice found Matthew 22:39, where Jesus says, "Love your neighbor as yourself." And Olivia read Romans 12:10, "Be devoted to one another in love. Honor one another above yourselves."

Though uncertain, neither Olivia nor Janice was fully ready to relinquish that flame or the solace it brought. They could only pray their light would continue guiding one another through the looming shadows of distrust.

CHAPTER 4
STRENGTH IN ADVERSITY

Saturdays were always busy at the Sunrise Diner, where Janice works. It is a cozy little place in the heart of town. It has that classic retro vibe with checkered floors, vintage booths, and a jukebox playing oldies in the corner. It is like stepping back in time. Janice dashed around the diner, balancing heavy trays of food and drinks in her hands. The lunch rush showed no signs of slowing down, and her feet ached from hours of being in motion. Wiping beads of sweat from her brow, Janice flashed an exhausted but warm smile at the customers.

"Enjoy your meal!" she called out as she delivered a plate of sizzling burgers and fries to a table of businessmen.

Janice does a little bit of everything. She takes orders, serves food with a smile, clears tables, and sometimes even helps in the kitchen when it gets busy. It can be challenging at times, especially when there is a rush, but she enjoys the fast-paced environment. Plus, it is always nice to see the regulars and have a little chat with them. It feels like a small community there.

As the afternoon dragged on, Janice's smile grew more strained. Her body felt weighed down by fatigue, but she persisted, determined to earn as many tips as possible for her grandmother. Once the rush finally eased, Janice slipped into the back kitchen for a brief respite. She leaned against the counter and closed her eyes, replaying Sunday's church service in her mind. Just thinking of her new friend, Olivia lifted Janice's spirits and filled her with gentle reassurance. She wondered what Olivia was doing.

When her break ended, Janice slipped her waitressing apron back on and got back to work. As customers pay their bills, many left sizeable tips for Janice's hard work. She gratefully pocketed the money, knowing it would go a long way in helping her grandmother pay the bills. Though exhausted after her double shift, Janice felt content that her efforts were making a difference for the woman who had given her a home. She looked forward to resting her sore feet and then seeing Olivia again at church the next morning, where they would surely find strength in each other.

Janice wearily unlocked the front door of the small home she shared with her grandmother. "Grammy, I'm home," she called out gently. A weak voice responded from the couch. Janice found her grandmother, Ruth, cradling a warm cup of tea, a knitted blanket pulled up to her chin.

"Oh Janice, there is my brave girl. How was work, dear?" Ruth asked through labored breaths. Her health had declined since the passing of Janice's grandpa, and she often struggled through bouts of illness.

Ruth Elizabeth Johnson, or Grammy, is truly the rock in Janice's life. She's a strong and resilient woman, just like Janice's parents were. She has this quiet strength about her that Janice has always admired.

Physically, Ruth has graying hair that she usually keeps in a neat bun, and her warm brown eyes always seem to hold so much wisdom. Her face may be lined with age, but her spirit is youthful and vibrant. She has had her fair share of hardships, especially taking on the responsibility of raising Janice after her parents passed away. Despite that, she has always been there for Janice, providing a loving and stable home. She has taught Janice the importance of perseverance, faith, and unconditional love.

She has a deep sense of spirituality and a strong connection to her faith. She has been a guiding light for Janice, helping her navigate through life's challenges while reminding her of the importance of humility and gratitude. Ruth is a hardworking woman, taking on odd jobs whenever she can to make ends meet. One must admire her work ethic and determination, even when times get tough. She has taught Janice the value of resilience and never giving up, no matter the circumstances.

"It was long but worth it," Janice replied, lightly kissing Ruth's wrinkled forehead. She noticed her grandmother's medicine bottles were untouched on the side table. "Have you taken your doses yet, Grammy?" At Ruth's head shake, Janice measured out the pills and helped raise her frail body to wash them down with sips of tea.

"My sweet Janice, always looking after me," Ruth sighed wearily once her medicine was swallowed. Janice gently laid her back down and tucked the blankets firmly around her shivering form.

"Get some rest now. I will start on dinner, okay?" Ruth smiled and clasped Janice's hand with weakened fingers.

"I don't know how I would manage without you, dear heart. You give this old soul so much strength."

Janice's eyes shone with tears of love for the woman who was her whole world. She stayed by Ruth's side, giving comfort until sleep claimed her weary grandmother. Once her breathing had evened out in sleep, Janice decided to hold off on dinner for now and quietly made her way to her tiny bedroom. She dug through her bedside drawer until her fingers closed around a worn photograph tucked inside.

Pulling it out, Janice studied the faded image of her parents on their wedding day. Mom's radiant smile and Dad's loving gaze never failed to stir bittersweet feelings within her. "I miss you both so much," Janice whispered into the dark room. So many years had passed since that terrible night when a drunk driver took them from this world. But Janice swore she could still feel her parents' spirits hovering near, giving her strength. "I try every day to make you proud," she said out loud, tracing their faces with a gentle finger. "Taking care of Grammy, working hard, making new friends..."

A smile crossed Janice's lips as she thought of Olivia.

Somewhere inside, she felt certain her parents would have loved Olivia's kind and insightful spirit. Clutching the photo close to her heart, Janice said a prayer of gratitude for the blessing of memories. Though adversity could knock her down, love would light the way forward and carry her faith even in the darkness.

No time for rest. Janice had to get ready to leave for the soup kitchen where she volunteers. Fortunately, it was a short walk to Hope's Kitchen. It is located in the heart of town, just a few blocks away from the main street. It is a warm and welcoming place that provides hot meals and support for those in need. Being able to lend a helping hand there brings Janice a sense of joy and fulfillment.

Janice stirred a large pot of simmering soup, filling the shelter kitchen with mouthwatering aromas. As a regular volunteer, she knew the flavors would provide comfort to the shelter patrons enduring life's difficulties. Soon, lines of people formed, bowls in hand. Janice smiled warmly and dished out servings with hearty scoops.

"There you go, enjoy!" she said, making eye contact with each person. Their stories of hardship stirred deep empathy within her soul. She connected with a father struggling to find work and house his family. "It will not always be this way; the ups will come," Janice assured him. At another table sat a shivering woman who had lost everything to addiction; Janice spoke to her with patience and care.

As Janice worked, she found solace in helping others through their suffering. Though immense challenges lay ahead, small acts of compassion lifted her spirit. Witnessing resilience in the face of true struggle also gave Janice a perspective on her own life. While pain existed, so did hope and humanity.

Before leaving, Janice bid the shelter residents farewell with warm embraces. She knew that in their smiles was strength, and her volunteer work was but a small repayment for life's abundant blessings. The experience of helping others brought Janice a sense of purpose and fulfillment like nothing else. While her own life had known deep sadness, she found joy in easing the struggles of people down on their luck. It did not matter that Janice bore hardships of her own as an orphan caring for her aging guardian; it just reaffirmed Janice's deep faith in goodness. Janice began the walk home, her mind filled with faces from the shelter.

Though exhaustion weighed heavily on her body after a long day of work and volunteering, her soul felt light; what mattered was the healing she could offer through compassion.

As she approached her small house, Janice smiled gently at the memories of gentle conversations over soup. Though darkness lingered for many, her interactions planted small seeds of hope. If she could lend an ear, alleviate hunger, or instill courage in just one person, it made Janice's sacrifices feel deeply meaningful.

Stepping through the doorway, Janice was greeted by her grandmother's loving gaze. She recounted portions of her day, glossing over her own weariness. Ruth smiled proudly at Janice's selflessness, knowing her dear girl possessed the heart and spirit to overcome any adversity.

After dinner, Janice helped her grandmother prepare for bed. She felt gratitude for life's blessings far outweighing its hardships. Her resilience was nourished by bringing light to others facing even greater challenges.

Meanwhile, Olivia lay on her bed, staring up at the ceiling with a sigh. Though comfortable and cared for, she had been feeling adrift lately without fully understanding why. While her family attended church and observed rituals, Olivia sometimes found the sermons lacking meaning. What was her greater purpose in this comfortable life? She envied how Janice seemed to have found fulfillment through her strong faith and selfless acts. Thinking of Janice volunteering at the shelter, Olivia smiled softly. Despite facing hardships unlike her own, Janice shone with inner confidence and compassion. While Olivia craved a deeper purpose, Janice embraced it wholeheartedly through helping others.

Perhaps there were lessons Olivia could learn about finding direction even in times of plenty. As with Janice, truly seeing beyond one's own circumstances might unlock life's gifts. She wished to better understand her friend's resilient spirit and to walk closer to Janice on her own journey of faith.

Lost in thought, Olivia gazed out at the setting sun. Its warm glow reminded her that even in doubt, light and beauty existed all around for those who looked with open eyes. Tomorrow, the church may provide renewed perspective through Janice's example of strength in adversity.

Sunday morning, Janice spotted Olivia waiting outside the church doors.

"Good morning!" she called out cheerily. Olivia smiled, sensing an inner radiance in her friend. As they sat on "their" bench, Janice recounted her Saturday volunteering at the shelter. Olivia listened intently, captivated by Janice's animated descriptions and obvious care for others.

"It is so fulfilling to help however I can," Janice said earnestly. Olivia was struck by Janice's passion.

"You have a gift for connecting with people in their toughest times," she noted kindly. Janice beamed at the praise but waved it off modestly.

"Will you join me next Saturday?" Janice proposed shyly. "The more hands we have, the better. And I think you would find it very rewarding."

Olivia grinned, flattered by Janice's trust. She was eager to learn from Janice's example and hopefully alleviate hardship herself. "I would love to," Olivia replied sincerely.

Happiness radiated from Janice, and Olivia felt her own heart swell in return. She looked forward to standing alongside her inspiring friend and opening her eyes to a world of untapped purpose. Their bond strengthened with each understanding shared.

As Olivia walked home, pondering their conversation, she realized with a jolt that she had made unfair assumptions about Janice's life. Beneath her friend's cheerful surface lay depths of resilience borne from immense challenges.

While Olivia saw comfort, Janice knew true hardship. Yet she radiated hope instead of despair. There were lessons in Janice's strength that Olivia felt privileged to learn. She replayed Janice's eager volunteering, her compassion for strangers, and caring for her ailing Grandmother. These were not superficial acts but reflections of Janice's selfless character. Olivia was just starting to grasp that, despite differences, within their hearts beat similarities.

Janice possessed depths Olivia had failed to see. But underneath her own comfortable shell lay curiosities about helping others, which Janice was helping cultivate. Their friendship was laying bare new perspectives and purposes each girl never expected to find. As Olivia gazed at the sunset, she sent thanks to kindred spirits who guided her outside preconceived notions. Her trust in Janice and faith in life's mysteries were growing stronger each day.

CHAPTER 5
SEEKING ANSWERS

Olivia shifted uncomfortably in the pew as Pastor Jonathon Thomas' sermon droned on. Normally, she listened passively, but today, restlessness stirred within her. Her mind wandered to discussions she and Janice had shared over the past few weeks.

Her friend spoke of faith with such sincere conviction, drawing strength from scripture in a way Olivia struggled to understand. While Janice faced immense challenges, her trust in God's plan remained unwavering. Olivia found herself questioning parts of Pastor Thomas' readings more deeply now.

A passage about God testing believers confused her, James 1:2-4. It says, "Consider it pure joy, my brothers and sisters, whenever you face trials of many kinds because you know that the testing of your faith produces perseverance. Let perseverance finish its work so that you may be mature and complete, not lacking anything." Did an omnipotent God truly need to test humanity's faith? And how could a loving God ordain suffering?

Pastor Thomas is passionate about his faith and dedicated to serving the congregation. He is a middle-aged man with a warm smile and a kind presence. When he speaks during sermons, his words are filled with wisdom and sincerity. He has a gentle yet confident demeanor that instantly puts people at ease. Pastor Thomas is a great listener and always takes the time to truly understand the concerns and needs of his flock. He is known for his thought-provoking sermons that challenge parishioners to think critically and apply their faith to our everyday lives. His genuine care for the community is evident, as he regularly organizes outreach programs and encourages participation in charitable endeavors. Above all, Pastor Thomas is a true leader, guiding people on their spiritual journeys and inspiring them to live out their faith in meaningful ways.

Olivia glanced at Janice sitting beside her. Peace radiated from Janice as she listened intently. Olivia wished she possessed even a fraction of that inner peace. How did

Janice reconcile life's hardships with her faith? After service was over, Olivia asked if Janice had time to chat.

As they walked along the church grounds, Olivia voiced her queries gently. "I don't mean to doubt, only to understand like you seem to," she said.

Janice smiled. "Doubt is natural. My faith grew from wrestling with life's mysteries, not avoiding them." She spoke of finding purpose in adversity by helping others, as her parents' memories lived on in good works. Though the road was long, God's light guided her step by step.

Olivia felt her spirit lift watching birds play in the trees. Janice's insights resonated within her, awakening her to faith's deeper meanings. She grasped now why this stunning girl beside her remained her rock.

Olivia said goodbye to Janice as she was waiting to speak with Pastor Thomas, who was finishing a conversation with another parishioner. When his conversation ended, she nervously approached. "Pastor, may I ask about some things that are troubling me?" He smiled warmly. "Of course, how can I help?" Olivia shared her discussions with Janice and questions arising from them. The pastor listened patiently and answered to the best of his understanding.

But his responses left Olivia still searching for deeper insight. He spoke of faith as the ultimate truth, not a journey of continuous learning. When she pressed on the nature of God and evil in the world, he fell back on it being a "mystery of faith."

Olivia went away, respecting Pastor Thomas but realizing his words could not quench her thirst for more profound answers. She saw faith as a seed needing sunlight and soil to sprout, not something fully formed from the start.

Her conversation affirmed Janice as someone who nurtured questioning rather than avoiding tricky issues. Olivia's trust in her understanding friend grew more, along with her certainty that together, they would find the enlightenment she sought. Olivia met up with Janice at the playground near the church.

"The pastor did not satisfy me," she burst out. "Do I take everything on faith alone?" Janice listened intently as Olivia relayed her conversation.

Instead of judging, Janice smiled. "Questioning shows wisdom. A thinking faith is richer than a passive one." Relief flooded Olivia. She expected rebuke for doubting, not praise for her courage.

"But what if my questions undermine my faith?"

"Doubt refines belief," Janice said gently. "Not knowing an answer is not lacking faith; it is leaving room for understanding to deepen. Our souls evolve through grappling with life's profoundest riddles." Olivia marveled at Janice's perspective. While her friend faced difficulties daily, Janice embraced challenges rather than fearing them.

Her resilience put Olivia further at ease. "You give me courage, Olivia. Pursue your inquiries freely; truth has nothing to fear from examination. And I will gladly listen, as always, to share in your discoveries."

Janice's unconditional support lifted Olivia's spirits. Their bond grew deeper through this moment of questioning and acceptance. More than ever, Olivia felt blessed by this singular soul.

Olivia sighed. "It is confusing separating what is doctrine and what is faith's essence."

"Indeed." Janice gazed at birds playing among branches. "I focus on faith's core: love, hope, compassion. Jesus taught kindness towards others. The mysteries do not trouble me." She turned to Olivia with a calm smile. "Who can say why life contains sorrow? I only know in darkness small acts of goodness are lights to guide our steps. Faith means embracing life fully, not avoiding its riddles."

Olivia pondered Janice's perspective. "But what about following rules exactly as written?"

"Christ seemed less rigid," Janice replied. "He offered mercy to those deemed sinful. Faith begins with an open hand, not a clenched fist." Her wisdom resonated within Olivia. Janice did not shrink from inquiry; she only saw mysteries as paths toward deeper empathy.

"You give me a truer glimpse of faith," Olivia said gratefully. Janice's example stirred her spirit like no scripture ever had, kindling hope of finding answers through lives touched with compassion. Olivia sensed their friendship blossoming with this sharing of insights, strengthening her budding journey.

The girls sat reflecting as a breeze rustled through the trees. Though varied in experience, each saw truths in the other's view. "You broaden my world," Janice said gently. "Life has presented me with hardship, yet through empathy, I find comfort. Watching you awakens hopes for education and chances I never dared dream."

Olivia nodded slowly. "And your resilience humbles me. I took family and security for granted while you fight daily with quiet courage. Now I see privileges require using advantage to aid others, not isolate myself."

"I think our bond shows that backgrounds can only divide if we let it happen," Janice continued. "Differences pale next to the lifelong questions drawing all souls upward: why suffer? How to love? Where to find purpose? Answering takes open eyes, and hands joined."

Peace filled the girls seeing new horizons open through each other's presence. Despite disparities, within their kindred spirits bloomed uplifting faith so all may gain footholds climbing to illumination.

Olivia walked home reflectively as the day pressed on. Companionship with Janice unlocked new depths in her ideas and spirit each day.

While others saw differences in class or faith, Janice saw only souls desiring light. Her calm acceptance stirred Olivia to ponder life from angles untouched before. Janice quietly empowered courage for questioning everything yet finding answers through compassion transcending all. Olivia meditated upon the day's conversations. Janice's wisdom flowed not from books alone but from experiences, molding her into a healer of souls. Seeing the past surface into the well of resilience under her friend's outer calm, Olivia grasped faith's eternal questions and engaged minds and hearts together most deeply.

She smiled, sending a prayer of thanks into gathering dusk. "May our friendship ever broaden both and grant serenity to those facing questions more perplexing than any reply."

By Janice's side, no mystery need bring fear; hand in hand two seekers will find relief, as through sharing life's beauty and sorrow, empathy shows mercy as the sole solution to all. With such faithful guidance, Olivia wonders what joy awaits in further unfoldings before them.

She walked on, mind and spirit opened like flowers drinking in light of the understanding blossoming between them.

Olivia sat pensively through dinner, replaying her day. Her parents remarked on her quiet thoughtfulness.

"Something on your mind, dear?" her mother asked.

Olivia took a breath. "I have been wrestling with my faith. Some church teachings do not resonate anymore."

Her father frowned. "What brought this on?"

She told of the conversation with the pastor, which had left her unfulfilled, and Janice's insightful perspective.

Her mother sighed. "Janice seems... troubled. It's best to focus inward and not let outside views shake your beliefs."

"But Janice enlightens me." Olivia pleaded for understanding. "Faith is not static; it evolves as we do."

"We only want you grounded, sweetheart," her father

added. "Don't let doubtful company steer you off course."

His implied criticism of Janice stung. Olivia wanted to defend her but saw only concern in their eyes. She loved and trusted her parents, yet their reaction saddened her. From them, she had found not wisdom but worry over her questioning spirit. Once more, Janice seemed to be her sole kindred soul in faith's unfolding journey.

That evening, Olivia retreated to her room, lost in thought. Her parents only meant well yet failed to grasp faith flourishing through inquiry.

She lay staring at shadows, pondering truths Janice had unveiled, inspiring hope despite life's darkness. Her friend embraced each doubt as she stepped towards a deeper light, not threats to be crushed. By contrast, well-meaning warnings of her parents now rang hollow and controlling.

Alone with swirling questions, Olivia missed Janice's calm presence most sorely. Janice affirmed dignity in facing mysteries freely, not fearing them in silence. While family loved, only Janice understood that faith required nourishment from within and without.

A lone tear glistened on Olivia's cheek. Family remained dear, yet on faith's journey, she must follow her heart's beckoning. Resolving to keep thoughts veiled henceforth from condemnation, she prayed for Janice's reassuring smile tomorrow. Their souls mingled on the same quest; together, each dawn, they would find solace facing uncertainties as Janice's empathy shone refuge amid life's fluctuations. In times of doubt, one true anchor lit her way, the steadfast radiance of a kindred spirit walking together into tomorrow.

CHAPTER 6
CHALLENGE FROM WITHIN

Olivia sat restlessly in the pew as Pastor Thomas' sermon droned on. While she used to soak in his wisdom, she now found herself questioning parts of the message.

Pastor Thomas stated that doubts were signs of a weak faith, referencing Proverbs 3:5-6, "Trust in the Lord with all your heart and lean not on your own understanding; in all your ways submit to him, and he will make your paths straight,"

Olivia could not stop herself from speaking up. "But isn't human to question?" she asked, drawing surprised looks from nearby parishioners. "How can we deepen our understanding without exploring what we do not know?"

Pastor Thomas cleared his throat, clearly taken aback. "Faith is about accepting truths, not debating them, my child. Doubts can undermine our devotion if given too much attention."

Olivia wanted to respond but held her tongue, noticing Betty and Martha shaking their heads disapprovingly. She spotted Janice giving her an encouraging nod, which calmed her irritation. Still, she felt restless, wondering how best to reconcile faith and free thinking.

After the service had ended, Olivia asked Janice about the exchange, worried it added more hostility toward their friendship. But Janice assured her that questioning led to richer beliefs. "Your inquisitiveness shows character, not flaws," Janice said.

Olivia smiled, thankful for Janice's acceptance. Yet she knew this incident added to the pressures they faced. While their bond grew stronger each Sunday, so did the criticism.

As Janice worked double shifts and Olivia battled her family, their friendship underwent its most strenuous test yet. Both drew courage from their loyal commitment, determined to stay true to the understanding they found in each other.

Olivia stormed into the house, still fuming from the confrontation at church. Her parents were waiting for her in the living room.

"We are not happy about what happened," said her father sternly. "You need to stop this rebellious behavior, Olivia. It is unladylike to question authority like that."

"But I was just…" Olivia started to protest.

Her mother cut her off. "You are upsetting the others with these antics. Can't you see you are disrupting things? Blending in is more important than voicing doubts." Olivia felt her anger rising but held her tongue. She knew arguing was pointless. Still, she believed challenging traditions was the only way to find truth.

As her parents continued lecturing, Olivia tuned them out. Her mind drifted to Janice, who understood her inquisitiveness and did not demand conformity. In those brief moments at church, she felt her most authentic self. Olivia values open-mindedness and the freedom to ask questions. Hearing her parents say her behavior was disruptive and that she should not question authority made her feel misunderstood. It forced her to question whether her

73

desire to explore and deepen her faith was seen as a disruption to others. It was a difficult moment for Olivia because she believed that questioning and seeking understanding was an important part of her spiritual journey. However, she also understands that her parents might have been concerned about the social expectations of the church community. It created an inner conflict between her longing to connect more deeply with her faith and the desire to respect her parents' wishes.

Olivia nodded absently as her parents spoke, but internally, she seethed at their closed-mindedness. More than ever, she appreciated Janice's acceptance and resolved to stay faithful to the spirit of inquiry her friend represented.

Olivia said she was going to take a walk. She sent a text to Janice, asking her to meet at their usual spot at the playground.

"Hey, are you doing okay?" Janice asked, concerned.

Olivia sighed. "My parents will not stop harping at me about what happened at church. They just want me to conform, not think for myself."

Janice nodded sympathetically. "It is not easy facing that pressure. But I admire your spirit; it is what first drew me to you."

A faint smile appeared on Olivia's face at the compliment. "Still, I feel bad complaining when you have it so much harder," she said. "You don't need my burdens, too."

"Don't worry about burdening me," Janice said gently. "We are in this together. Your friendship means more to me than any chore or comment ever could."

Olivia was touched. "You always know what to say to lift my mood," she said gratefully. "Just being with you helps me feel less alone. Our friendship gives me strength to keep challenging norms in my own way."

Janice beamed at Olivia's faith in her. "You do the same for me each day," she said. "Now, tell me more. I'm always here to listen."

Olivia noticed Janice seemed troubled. "What's wrong?" she asked.

Janice sighed. "It's my grandma. She has not been well, and the doctor's bills keep coming. I have been working so much, but it still does not feel like enough."

Olivia took her hand comfortingly. "I am so sorry. Is there anything I can do to help?"

"No, you being here is help enough." Janice smiled gratefully. "Some nights, I worry we will lose our home. But then I think of you and feel like as long as we have each other, everything will be okay."

"You will never lose me," Olivia assured her. She wished she could ease Janice's burden somehow. "You work so hard yet stay so strong. I admire your resilience."

Janice nodded. "When times are tough, my faith gives me courage. All I can do is keep praying and give it my all at the diner. Some days that is a struggle, though."

Olivia squeezed her hand. "You're not alone in the struggle. I am here for you always, as you are for me. Together, we can face any hardship."

Olivia and Janice walked together in silence, both lost in thought. Finally, Olivia spoke. "I don't want you worrying about me and my silly problems. You carry so much as it is."

Janice shook her head. "Don't say that. Your challenges are just as real, even if they are different than mine. We are in this together, remember?"

"I know, but..." Olivia trailed off sighingly. "I don't like adding to your burdens. You do so much already."

Janice stopped and took both of Olivia's hands in hers. "Look at me. We support each other through everything. That is what true friendship means. I do not want you bottling things up to protect me."

Olivia blinked away tears, touched. "You are right. I just admire your strength so much. I do not want you to break under pressure."

A smile formed on Janice's lips. "As long as we have each other, neither of us will break. Now, come on, cheer up. Our bond gives me hope to face any storm."

Janice, still holding Olivia's hands, asked if she would pray with her.

Olivia said, "Of course," then they closed their eyes, and Janice prayed for strength and guidance. She prayed for the courage to face their individual struggles and to find comfort and peace in their faith. She also prayed for each other, asking for support and understanding in their friendship. It was a moment of vulnerability and connection, where they sought solace and hope together in prayer.

When Janice finished, she noticed Olivia was crying. "You always know how to lift my spirits. Thank you for standing by my side, as I will forever stand by yours."

Olivia told Janice that she wanted to go to the church to see if Pastor Thomas was there. She promised to call Janice later. They hugged, and Olivia walked to the church.

Pastor Thomas saw Olivia enter the church and approached. "May we speak privately?" he asked gently. Olivia's heart sank, anticipating a lecture.

Pastor Thomas sighed. "I understand questioning your faith, but it causes disturbance. Best keep such thoughts to God and yourself."

She felt tears welling. Not joyful tears like with Janice. "All I want is truth and purpose, not platitudes. Why should faith demand silence over understanding?"

The pastor laid a hand on her shoulder. "I know this is difficult, but some traditions must be honored to maintain community. Have faith that God's plan is wiser than you know."

Olivia bit her cheek, fighting the urge to argue. She knew any further outbursts would only isolate her further. "Thank you for your concern," she said politely.

"I will pray on your guidance." He nodded and left.

Alone, Olivia let angry tears fall, cursing the rigid rules suppressing her quest. More than ever, she longed for Janice's reassuring smile and acceptance of her independent spirit. Olivia wandered the streets before heading home, lost in turbulent thoughts.

Once home, her parents' disapproval weighed on her. She quickly went to her room and shut the door, trying to calm her swirling mind. After dinner, Olivia went for a long walk.

By dusk, she found herself at the edge of town, past neighborhoods into wooded greenery. A lone figure caught her eye, Janice, sitting pensively by a stream. At Olivia's approach, Janice turned with a surprised smile. "What are you doing out here?" she asked, patting the ground invitingly.

Olivia sighed and sat. "Escaping my parents' stares. I feel torn between staying true to myself and keeping the peace. It is a struggle to keep bottling up my beliefs."

Janice nodded understandingly. "Change is never easy, especially against rigid minds. But speaking your truth honors your journey, even if others do not see."

Olivia leaned gratefully against her friend. *How can someone the same age as me be so much wiser?* Thought Olivia and then said, "You always know just what to say. I wish the others understood that inquiring is not defiance but seeking. As long as I have your support, I will keep walking my path."

Janice put an arm around her shoulders. "And you have that support forever. Now come, the stars are beautiful tonight. Let's find comfort from our problems in the light of the stars."

As they lay back on the grass, Olivia gazed up at the night sky as the first stars emerged. She was glad Janice was with her, as her calming presence always soothed her frazzled thoughts.

But Janice had her own struggles tonight, caring for her ailing grandmother. Olivia wished she could ease that burden as Janice did so selflessly for her. A shooting star streaked across the inky darkness. Olivia closed her eyes, sending a silent prayer for Janice's strength and guidance on her path. No matter the hostility surrounding them, she believed their loyalty to each other could endure any trial.

As more stars illuminated the velvet sky, Olivia took comfort in the fact that Janice surely looked at these same celestial lights. Even when they were apart, their kindred spirits remained connected across the darkness. In Janice, Olivia had found a light to brighten her way during doubting times. And for that faith and friendship, she was eternally grateful.

After a while, with renewed hope in their hearts, Olivia and Janice rose and began the walk home, soothed by the thought of seeing each other again. Their journey together was only the beginning.

CHAPTER 7
CHALLENGE FROM WITHOUT

Whispers and hisses of "weirdo" and "charity case" followed Olivia and Janice as they walked the halls in their respective schools. Janice tried her best to ignore the cruel words, keeping her head down and eyes forward. She had endured difficult times before and learned that showing a reaction is what the bullies want.

It was more complicated for Olivia, though, as this was unfamiliar territory for her. The hurtful remarks stung deeply. At lunch, Olivia sat by herself, still upset by the morning's events. She watched enviously as other friends chatted and laughed together, wishing Janice was there. Just then, a shadow fell over her table. Olivia looked up to see two of the girls who had tormented her earlier.

"Aww, does the little baby need her charity friend to hold her hand?" one taunted.

"I would tell her to stay away from you if I were her. Wouldn't want her poorness to rub off," sneered the other.

Olivia bit her lip, fighting back tears. Before she could respond, a teacher intervened and sent the girls away with a warning. But the damage was done. Olivia fought the urge to flee, knowing Janice would tell her that was what the bullies wanted. She took a shaky breath and persisted with her lunch alone.

During history class, Olivia tried her best to focus on the lesson. But from behind her, she heard whispers and giggles from the same girls who had taunted her at lunch. "I cannot believe Olivia hangs out with that raggedy Janice," one sneered.

"Have you seen what she wears? So unfashionable."

"And her hair is always in such a messy bun—no effort at all. I do not know what Olivia sees in her," agreed another.

Olivia's hands balled into fists under her desk. She wanted nothing more than to whirl around and tell them how wrong they were. But she knew that would only invite more tormenting, so she stayed silent and fought back tears.

At the same time, at her school, Janice was in art class, sketching a landscape. She moved almost robotically, blocking out the quiet comments she heard behind her.

"Janice, the charity case... I wonder if she showers, let alone has a decent outfit." "Some girls have no fashion sense. At least she has her grandmother to do her hair for her, not that it would help."

Janice's eyes grew blurry with unshed tears as she continued drawing, giving no outward reaction to their cruel words. Inside, though, their insults reopened the wounds from her difficult past. She wished Olivia was there to give her strength.

Meanwhile, Olivia picked at her food, no longer hungry due to the tight knot of hurt in her stomach. Around her, the chatter and laughter of other students grated on her nerves. She could feel their eyes boring into her as rumors were swapped.

During Janice's lunch, she sat alone as well, chewing her lip raw. She kept her head down, not daring to meet any gaze for fear of what she might see there. All around, hushed voices and muffled chuckles drifted to her ears, but she refused to show curiosity about their reasons.

Both girls felt increasingly isolated as the week dragged on. During classes, transitioning to the next classes and study hall, whispers and giggles followed in their wake. Olivia and Janice developed a practiced disregard, pretending not to notice the torment surrounding them.

At the end of the day, Olivia and Janice met at the playground, as usual. Olivia walked slowly to their meeting spot, toes dragging in the dirt. When Janice came into view, her red-rimmed eyes and slumped shoulders told of her despair. Seeing one another brought them immense relief. Their bond remained a light, as the whispers threatening to engulf them in darkness grew louder.

One look at Olivia's red eyes and Janice enveloped her in a hug. "I am here," was all she said, but it was precisely what Olivia needed to hear. In that moment, their friendship proved stronger than any torment their peers could inflict. Inside, though, the emotional wounds festered. Olivia missed Janice's comforting presence. Janice yearned for Olivia's strength and understanding. Only their friendship sustained them through these trials.

"Oh, Olivia," Janice gasped, pulling her into an embrace.

Olivia's dam broke, and she sobbed into Janice's shoulder. "I am s-sorry," Olivia hiccupped. "This is all m-my fault. You are g-getting hurt because of m-me."

Janice tightened her arms reassuringly. "Don't blame yourself. Their words mean nothing."

"But it is not f-fair!" Olivia wailed. "You d-don't deserve this."

"True strength lies in rising above petty insults," Janice soothed. "I've endured much worse. As long as we have each other, their small minds cannot touch us."

Olivia took a shuddering breath, comforted. "You always know j-just what to say."

Janice smiled softly. "That is what friends are for. Now come, dry your eyes. The bullies have stolen enough of our joy."

Hand in hand, the girls walked through the playground and into the park. United in sisterhood, their bond transcended the whispers seeking to break them. In each other, they found solace from the storms of intolerance.

That night, Olivia sank onto her bed with an exhausted sigh. She was not ready to face the onslaught of questions from her parents. Sure enough, a soft knock sounded before her mother peeked in.

"Olivia, darling, are you alright?" Olivia nodded weakly. Her mother entered, father in tow, and sat beside her. "We heard about the rumors at school. Are the other girls giving you trouble?"

"Because of Janice?" her father added gently. Olivia tensed.

"It is not her fault. They just don't understand our friendship." Her parents exchanged a look. "We worry it may damage your reputation, being associated with her," her mother said.

Olivia sat up straight. "That is unfair! Janice is the truest friend I have known. I won't abandon her to please gossip."

Her father squeezed her shoulder. "We only want what is best for you, sweetheart. Think about whether continuing this friendship brings more pain than joy."

As they left, Olivia's eyes burned with tears. Janice was her rock; she could not betray her now. Their friendship was worth any hardship. She prayed the tide would turn so their love could shine through once more.

Janice hurried to her shift at the diner, dreading the Friday night crowd. Drunks usually meant rude remarks under the guise of humor. She tied on her apron and straightened her nametag, steeling herself. The dinner rush soon began, relentless orders flying her way. Janice moved fast despite the harshness of jeers and catcalls.

"Hey, sweetheart, how 'bout a smile with that coffee?" yelled a bleary-eyed patron.

"Think she could afford new clothes if she charged for those long legs?" guffawed another.

Janice gritted her teeth and kept her face pleasant. She had learned that ignoring such behavior denied the satisfaction they craved. As the night wore on, sleazy comments grew bolder. A burly man grabbed her wrist. "C'mere honey, gimme a kiss!"

Janice yanked free, voice steady. "I must get back to work, sir."

Despite adversity, Janice persevered with grace and poise, serving each customer with equal care. Her maturity humbled onlookers. By shift's end, her patrons' crudeness seemed small compared to Janice's shining spirit. She counted her tips, proud to help provide for her grandmother once more.

Janice wearily walked home and entered, glad to be home, exhausted after her long shift. The phone was ringing as she entered.

"Hello?"

"Janice, it is me," came Olivia's voice, comforting as a warm hug. Janice sank into a chair with a sigh.

"How was your night?"

"Dull without you," Olivia said softly.

"I missed hearing about your day." Though equally tired, Janice brightened, launching into an account of the diner antics. She spun them in an amusing light, bringing Olivia's first smile all week.

"You always seem to find the humor," Olivia remarked with admiration.

"Laughter helps more than anger," Janice replied wisely. Olivia told of her quiet evening, feeling uplifted just speaking to her dear friend again. They avoided mentioning the toxicity at school, instead discussing hopes for a brighter future.

As the sky darkened, their conversation became drowsy murmurs of comfort. Though apart, their bond shone through the phone, a reminder that, together or separate, they had each other's support during hard times. With Janice's soothing tone in her ear, Olivia drifted to sleep feeling secure in their eternal friendship. The week had taken a toll on Olivia and Janice. Yet their Sunday meeting at church held more anticipation than dread.

Catching sight of each other, worry lines faded into smiles. Janice's gentle hug soothed Olivia's frazzled nerves. Together, they entered the quiet sanctuary, seeking its peace. During the service, Martha's glare and Betty's chuckling became background noise. The girls focused on their bond instead of judgments.

After, they walked amid a sea of whispers without hearing a word. Olivia sighed. "Sometimes I wish they could see you as I do, the kindest soul I know."

Janice squeezed her hand. "Their opinions don't define our worth. If we have each other, nothing can penetrate."

Olivia nodded, comforted. "You're right. Our friendship is stronger than their small minds. Whatever trials come, we will endure through loyalty and love."

With that, they continued walking, unaware that behind them, Betty watched thoughtfully. Perhaps these girls possessed wisdom beyond her closed views. For now, Olivia and Janice simply enjoyed the support they found together, braving life's tests as a united team.

CHAPTER 8
TOUCHING LIVES

The hurtful words echoed in their minds throughout the next day at school. When classes ended, Olivia hurried to the playground, their spot, hoping Janice would already be there waiting for her. Janice arrived soon after, and they embraced, finding consolation in each other's presence.

"Their words mean nothing," Janice soothed. "We know the truth." Still, Olivia wished she could do something, anything, to help others feel less alone.

"What if we volunteered at the homeless shelter this weekend?" she suggested. Janice's face lit up.

"What a wonderful idea. Let's go together."

When Olivia suggested going to the shelter with Janice, Janice felt a mixture of surprise and gratitude. It was really touching to see Olivia's willingness to step out of her comfort zone and join her in helping others. It made Janice appreciate their friendship even more, knowing that she genuinely cared about making a positive impact in the world.

The following Saturday, they arrived at the shelter. Janice was familiar with the routine of helping in the kitchens. Olivia joined, eager to learn. They worked tirelessly, serving warm meals to the patrons. Their resilience struck Olivia. Though circumstances had brought them low, their humanity remained.

During a break, Olivia turned to Janice. "I understand now what sustains your faith, seeing strength in adversity and goodness in people, no matter their lot in life."

Janice took Olivia's hand. "You have a kind heart. These experiences will stay with you, for better or worse, but at least we walk this path side by side."

Their efforts were appreciated. At the end of their shift, the shelter director thanked them. The patrons also expressed gratitude. One man said Janice's smile each week lifted his spirits. As they departed, Olivia felt a sense of purpose blossom within her soul. This, she realized, was what faith meant: touching lives and finding light even in darkness.

That Monday, the cruelty continued at their schools. During English, Olivia overheard two girls snickering about Janice's shabby clothes and unstylish hair. She slammed her book shut, glaring at them, but said nothing.

At her school, Janice walked calmly to her seat, though inside, she ached. A group of boys leaned against the lockers. "Look who showed up in rags today," one jeered. Janice stared ahead, eyes fogging with the hurt she refused to show.

That afternoon, they met at the playground as usual. "I am so sorry about what they said," Olivia whispered, embracing her.

But Janice just smiled sadly. "Their words can't hurt me, not when we have each other."

Still, Olivia wished she could shield Janice from such cruelty. An idea came to her. "We should go shopping this weekend. My treat. You can choose whatever you like."

Janice shook her head politely. "I can't let you do that..."

"Please, it would make me happy. And you deserve every kindness, my dearest friend."

Janice saw the sincerity in Olivia's eyes and relented. A smile broke through. "Then, I accept. Thank you, Liv." Hand in hand, they left the playground. The insults no longer mattered as much, faced with such unconditional love and acceptance.

On Friday, as Olivia sat alone at lunch, she tried to ignore the whispers and giggles around her. From another table, she heard her and Janice's name between bites of food, followed by cruel laughter. She stared hard at her sandwich, fighting angry tears. At her own lonely table across town, Janice steadily worked through her meal, pretending not to notice people pretending to whisper behind their hands. She concentrated on the sunlight filtering through the trees at the playground, where Olivia would be waiting as always.

When the bells finally rang at both schools, the girls hurried to their sanctuary, falling into a tight embrace as soon as they reached the playground. Neither needed to say the hurtful things they had endured alone that day. They simply took comfort in one another, knowing that together, somehow, they would endure this too. Their isolation grew, but so did their bond. Faced with cruelty, their friendship blossomed more beautifully, a testament to the power of pairing compassion against indifference. Side by side, they took strength and found light even in the shadows of solitude.

But then, out of nowhere, Olivia burst into tears, "I am so sorry," she sobbed. "This is all my fault."

Janice pulled her into a gentle embrace. "What are you apologizing for?"

"The bullying and gossip. It is because of me and our friendship. You are suffering, and I hate it."

Janice took Olivia's hands in hers. "Look at me. I could never regret our friendship, no matter what petty things people say. Their words mean nothing to me."

"But they hurt you."

"Only because I see how they affect you. As long as we have each other, their opinions do not matter. We know the truth of who we are and what we share."

Janice brushed tears from Olivia's cheek. "Do not ever think you alone are responsible for my happiness! Our bond is a choice we both make, and I choose it gladly every day. Okay?"

Olivia nodded, hugging Janice again in gratitude. She was right. As long as they had this friendship, no torment could shake them. Their faith in each other was stronger than any cruelty the outside world could inflict.

That evening, over dinner, Olivia's parents brought up Janice once more. "We are worried this friendship is impacting you socially," her mother said gently. "Perhaps some distance would help smooth things over."

Olivia's jaw clenched. "After everything Janice and I have been through this week because of small-minded gossip, you want me to abandon her?"

"Your mother only means that concessions may need to be made," her father reasoned. "Reputations are fickle at your age."

"I won't betray my friend to appease hypocrites. Janice is worth any cost to my fleeting popularity. She has stayed by my side through every insult, and I won't do any less for her."

"We understand loyalty," said her mother. "Just consider if pursuing this is truly wise long term. Now, eat your dinner before it gets cold."

Olivia pushed her food around silently. No one understood Janice like she did. Their friendship was enduring truth, not a fad to be swayed by shallow opinions. She would remain devoted; it did not matter whatever social waves flowed around them.

On Saturday, Janice worked her shift at the diner as usual. "Table 6 needs refills," the manager barked. Janice weaved expertly between customers, balancing heavy trays. At one booth, a group of intoxicated men leered.

"Hey, sweetheart, what time you off? I will show you a real good time."

She ignored them calmly. "Enjoy your food, sir. Table 6, here are your drinks."

As the crowd grew rowdier, more jeers were thrown her way. But Janice persevered with poise, focusing on patrons who treated her with basic humanity. She thought of Olivia and the goodness that sustained her perseverance amid the darkness.

By the end of the long shift, she was drained. But leaving, she overheard a regular say, "That girl has got more character in her pinky than those drunks got in their whole bodies."

She smiled to herself, warmed by small acts of light among shadows. Such cruelty could not diminish Janice, for her strength lay not in things as fleeting as popularity or appearance but in virtues as steadfast as compassion and courage. With those guides, no torment could leave her weakened for long.

That night, as soon as Janice dragged herself home, she heard the phone ring. "Olivia," she smiled, answering. "Hi, Janice. I hoped I would catch you. How was work?"

Janice sighed. "The usual customers. But some days, their rude remarks do not hurt as much, thanks to kind souls like the man at Table 6."

"You are so strong, handling it all with grace," Olivia said earnestly.

Janice laughed. "I could say the same of you. Are the whispers at school any better?"

"Not really. But it doesn't matter what they say, as long as we have each other." Silence fell as they both considered another week facing torment alone.

Then Janice said lightly, "Look on the bright side, at least it is the weekend! We can sleep in."

Olivia smiled. Trust Janice to focus on hope, even amid darkness. "You always know how to lift my mood. Thank you, my dearest friend."

"Anytime. Goodnight, Liv. See you at church."

Hanging up, Olivia felt anchored, knowing Janice was on the other end of the line, a strong yet gentle soul who understood her perfectly. Their bond gave her quiet courage to face each challenging day. Olivia reached for her Bible, looking to see what it said about friendship.

She found a couple of verses that really resonated with her: Proverbs 17:17, "A friend loves at all times, and a brother is born for a time of adversity." This verse reminds her of the true essence of friendship, which is about standing by each other through the good times and the tough times. Another verse she found was Ecclesiastes 4:9-10, "Two are better than one because they have a good return for their labor: If either of them falls down, one can help the other up." Olivia realized this verse emphasizes the importance of having a supportive friend who can lift you up when you are down. These verses gave her comfort and inspired her to cherish the friendship she has with Janice. With that, she drifted off to sleep.

The following day, as Olivia and Janice entered the church hand in hand, they felt eyes upon them, judging. But after all they had endured that brutal week together, such stares meant little. They took their seats, leaning close to share hushed words and soft smiles.

"Our outer faces may fade in others' opinions," Janice murmured. "But the truth we know within is changeless."

Olivia squeezed her hand. "You're right. Their perspectives can't outweigh what really matters: our bond, which grows only deeper through each test. As long as we have faith in each other, no cruelty can shake us."

The flickering flames of prejudice danced harmlessly by. For the light of their friendship, kindled from understanding in adversity, could not be diminished by shadows from small minds. It would endure, and with its guidance, so would they, walking together in courage towards whatever might come and finding solace where once there was only loneliness and isolation.

Their journey, once meant to divide, had instead brought them into the closest of unions. And though tribulation stalked their steps, its fruits enriched their lives all the more for withstanding every challenge, side by radiant side.

CHAPTER 9
FALLING OUT

Olivia spotted Janice sitting on their usual bench in the playground. Something seemed off as Janice stared intently at the ground, lost in troubled thoughts.

"Hey, is everything okay?" Olivia asked, sitting down next to her friend. Janice looked up with a half-hearted smile.

"I'm alright. Just feeling a bit tired today, I guess."

Olivia frowned. "Don't pretend everything is fine when it's not. We said we would be honest with each other, remember?"

Sighing, Janice laid her head on Olivia's shoulder. "It has been a long week. Work has been rough, with my boss breathing down my neck. And the other girls will not stop with their cruel jokes."

"I am so sorry," Olivia said softly. "It can't be easy dealing with all that on your own. You know you are not alone, right? I am here for you."

Janice lifted her head. "I know. And I really appreciate your support. But I am worried this friendship is putting too much pressure on you. You don't deserve the backlash from everyone just for being my friend."

Olivia shook her head firmly. "Don't ever say that! Our friendship means everything to me." She took Janice's hands in hers. "I just want you to feel like you can share your burdens with me. No more pretending, okay?"

Janice smiled weakly. "No more pretending. I promise."

They sat in silence for a while, finding comfort in each other's company as the sun began to sink low in the sky. Janice stared at her hands. "I am trying, Olivia, I really am. It is just hard sometimes, pretending everything is fine when it is not."

A frown crept onto Olivia's face. "At least you don't have parents constantly pressuring you to be someone you are not."

Scoffing, Janice looked up at Olivia. "What do you know about pressure? You have always had everything handed to you on a silver platter."

Anger flashed in Olivia's eyes. "Don't talk like you know what my life is like. You have no idea what it is like dealing with their expectations every day."

Janice stood up abruptly. "I'm sorry my struggles are such an inconvenience for you, Princess. Must be hard having maids and money."

Olivia rose, too, glaring at Janice. "Do not call me that. You think you are the only one with problems? Try living up to their perfect image of you 24/7 with no room for mistakes."

Their voices rose in volume, thick with hurt and frustration. Olivia accused Janice of arrogance, while Janice shot back, stating that Olivia was ungrateful. All the pain and pressure they had bottled up came spilling out in a torrent of barbed words. Chests heaving, they fell silent, regret swirling in with anger. Janice frowned, tears brimming in her eyes.

"You are always questioning things, never satisfied with what is given. Unlike some, I am grateful for my faith."

Olivia seethed, fists clenched. "All I want is answers, not blind obedience like you. You must think I am so naïve."

Hurt flashed across Janice's face. "And you think so little of where I come from. Like my struggles don't even matter next to your existential crisis!" Their voices had risen to shouts that echoed in the empty playground. All the pain, fear, and doubt they had kept bottled within themselves for weeks now came gushing out. Olivia accused Janice of judging her quest for deeper understanding. Janice shot back that Olivia looked down on her hard life. Their insecurities, exacerbated by weeks of bullying and scrutiny, boiled over in a torrent of lashing words.

Tears streamed down Janice's face now, cheeks flushed with anger and shame. "You just don't understand," Olivia snarled.

Janice sank to the ground and sobbed, any lingering hope for reconciliation crushed under the weight of their seething emotions. All the joy their friendship had offered was now ripped away, leaving two solitary souls in its place. Olivia wiped furiously at her eyes, trying to stem the flow of tears.

"I can't do this anymore, Janice. I just can't."

"Can't do what?" Janice asked desperately, tears still dripping onto the cracked asphalt.

"Us!" Olivia cried. "I am so tired of fighting everyone and everything, including you sometimes, of trying to be something I am not."

Janice reached for her hand, but Olivia yanked it away. "I am not your project to fix, okay? I don't need you analyzing me and my faith all the time."

"That is not what I am trying to do," Janice begged. "I just want to understand."

"Well, stop!" Olivia screamed, her voice echoing off the empty courtyard walls. "I cannot keep trying to live up to everyone's rules, my parents, the church, even you!"

Olivia took a shuddering breath, glaring furiously at Janice through reddened eyes. "I thought you were different. But you are all the same, pushing and pushing until I break.

Well, I broke a long time ago, Janice, and there is no fixing me now."

With that painful confession, Olivia spun on her heel and ran, sobs tearing from her chest as she fled from the remains of their shattered friendship.

Janice collapsed anew, her heart splintering with every one of Olivia's agonized cries.

Olivia burst through the front door of her home, tears pouring down her face. "Mom!" she cried, crumbling into her mother's embrace. "Shh, it is okay, sweetheart. What happened?"

Between sobs, Olivia choked out, "Janice, we fought and said awful things. I lost my best friend because of my stupid mouth!"

Her mother rubbed her back gently. "I know it hurts now, but some friendships just are not meant to last."

Olivia looked up, eyes puffy and red. "But it is not fair! I love her."

Sighing, her mother placed a hand on her cheek. "I know you care about her. But you two come from such different worlds. It was never going to be easy."

"But we understood each other. Now I am all alone," Olivia wept.

Her mother hugged her tightly. "You will get through this. And who knows, maybe in time you can both forgive and learn from this experience." Olivia nodded, even as a fresh wave of hurt washed over her. Clinging to her mother, she cried for all the beautiful moments with Janice that were now lost to the cruelty of their harsh words.

Janice walked slowly down the empty street, cheeks still wet from crying. She replayed their fight over and over in her head, pounding each word further into her bruised heart.

How could I be so stupid, pushing Olivia when she was already at her limit? Janice thought miserably. Some friend I am.

A car drove by, and Janice shrank into herself, feeling exposed in her sorrow. What was once a comfort, this street now seemed menacing in the fading daylight. As her grandmother's house came into view, Janice halted. She was not ready to face more hurt, to see the disappointment in her grandmother's eyes at the failure of her friendship, a friendship that had brought fleeting joy to Janice's solitary life. Now, she was alone again, without even Olivia's gentle smile to stave off the dark.

Kicking a stone, Janice remembered Olivia's tearful face, and another sob racked her body. *How could one argument shatter what they had so carefully built? All the light and care their bond had offered, now snuffed out by careless, cutting words.* Janice hugged herself tightly against the deepening chill, both within and without.

As she wept under the dimming stars, Janice prayed for Olivia, for herself, and for the lost hope of reconciliation between two broken souls.

The days that followed dragged endlessly for Olivia and Janice. Olivia found herself constantly looking for a familiar face in the crowd, only to be met with emptiness. She replayed their fight obsessively, wanting to take back the hurtful words but too proud to reach out first.

Janice immersed herself in work and school, if only to drown out thoughts of laughter and insight shared with her dearest friend. Each chime of the doorbell made her foolishly hope that Olivia had come before cold reality set in again.

At night, they lay awake, longing for easier times and the comfort of each other's embrace. Olivia wondered if Janice missed her at all or if she now saw her as spiteful and shallow. Janice debated sending a text, an olive branch to mend what had broken. But fear and shame held her back. *What if Olivia wanted nothing more to do with the source of her pain?*

As another sleepless night dragged on, Janice gazed up at the stars and prayed. For forgiveness, for strength, and that somehow the rift between them could be healed. Olivia, too, stared into the darkness, wishing with all her heart that she could see Janice's smile once more.

Sunday morning, Olivia dragged herself to the church service with heavy feet. She glanced hopefully towards Janice's usual pew, only to find it empty. Her heart constricted at the sight, wounds still far too raw. Janice skipped church for the first time, unable to bear being in the same hallowed walls where their friendship had blossomed. She wept on her grandmother's shoulder, grieving all they had lost.

As the days passed in isolation, Janice wondered if she and Olivia could ever again find comfort and relief in each other's company or if their bond had been shattered beyond repair by hasty, hurtful words. Olivia replayed each snippet of their friendship on a loop, clinging to precious memories as physical reminders of Janice faded. She longed to erase the pain but sensed the damage ran too deep. Two solitary souls existed where once there was inseparable unity. Though their fallout had brought nothing but sorrow, attempting reconciliation now seemed fruitless, a fresh torment upon tender hearts.

All they could do was endure the desolation and hope that, in time, forgiveness might transform agony into understanding between them once more. For now, two hearts bled alone in the aftermath of a shattering they had never imagined possible.

CHAPTER 10
HEALING BEGINS

The school bell rang, signaling the start of the lunch period. Olivia slowly packed up her books and joined the swarm of students in the hallway. She kept her head down, trying to avoid making eye contact with anyone. As she walked to the cafeteria, she overheard cruel giggles and whispered all around her.

"Where is your friend Janice?" one voice sneered. "Are you too good for her now?" another taunted. Olivia's hands curled into fists, but she swallowed her anger and kept walking. She spent lunch alone at an empty table, pointedly ignoring the stares burning into her back. On the surface, she appeared calm, but inside, a storm was raging.

She missed Janice more than she could say. Every day without her friend hurt like a fresh wound that would not heal. Olivia replayed their fight over and over in her head, lingering on the hurtful words they had hurled at each other.

If only she could take it all back.

After the final bell, Olivia quickly packed up and left school, eager to escape to the solitude of the park. She wandered aimlessly for hours, lost in tumultuous thoughts. The setting sun painted the sky in hues of orange and pink, mirroring the whirlwind of emotions within her.

As darkness fell, Olivia sat on 'their' bench at the playground, gazing up at the stars, finding comfort in their distant beauty. A light breeze stirred, rustling the leaves with a sound like whispered prayers. At that moment, Olivia sent up a silent plea for forgiveness, understanding, and the healing of her fractured friendship with Janice. She silently quoted Ephesians 4:32, "Be kind to each other, tenderhearted, forgiving one another, just as God through Christ has forgiven you."

Tears welled up as she remembered Janice's smile, her calming presence, and the comfort they found in each other. Olivia knew only Janice could heal the aching wound in her heart. But would Janice ever want to see her again after the cruel things they had said? Olivia hugged her knees, wishing with all her soul that somehow their friendship could be repaired.

Olivia tried to hold back her tears as she walked home, but as soon as she entered her room, they began to fall freely. She collapsed on her bed and sobbed into her pillow, wetting the case with an ocean of regret and longing.

All the hurts and anxieties of the past weeks came pouring out in a torrent of emotions. Most of all, she ached for Janice's comforting embrace and the peace they found in each other. After some time, her tears subsided into sniffles. Olivia dug through her drawer to find a pen and paper. In the fading daylight, she poured her heart out in a letter to Janice.

"Dear Janice," it began. "I am so sorry for what I said during our fight. I did not mean any of it. You have been nothing but kind to me from the start. Please believe that you are not alone; I am here for you as much as you have been there for me."

Olivia wrote about how much Janice's friendship meant and how she was the only person who truly understood her struggles. She vowed to be open and listen without judgment from now on. By the time she finished, the sun had set, and shadows filled the room. Olivia re-read the letter, hoping Janice could find it in her heart to forgive her. But she lacked the courage to send it, fearing further

115

rejection. For now, she could only hope that someday, they might heal their bond.

Janice walked slowly through the empty cemetery, wilting flowers in hand. The setting sun cast long shadows as she made her way between the headstones, eyes trained on a familiar carved marker up ahead. She knelt before the two graves, tenderly placing the new flowers in the vases. Tracing her fingers over her parents' names, Janice broke down in tears. "I am so sorry, Mama, Papa," she sobbed. "I have let you both down."

Between gasps, Janice told them everything: how she pushed away the only friend who truly understood her, how much Olivia meant to her, and the cruel words they had exchanged. Her parents had taught her about kindness, and she had failed to show it when it mattered most. The chill of the gathering night sank into her bones, but Janice did not notice the cold. She stayed by the graves long after dusk fell, spilling her regrets in the moonlight. "I promise to do better," she whispered. "To be more understanding like you taught me. Please... give me a way to make things right with Livy again."

Finally spent, Janice dried her tears and got up unsteadily. As she left the cemetery, she sent up a prayer to her parents on the breeze for wisdom, compassion, and a path forward to heal the bond she treasured most.

Janice wearily entered Westside Community Church for Sunday service. Though she had avoided it for weeks for fear of running into Olivia, stepping inside still filled her with a sense of comfort and home. She attended services this morning without her grandmother, who was not feeling well and chose to stay home and rest.

She slid into the back pew as the service began, hoping to go unnoticed. But Janice soon spotted old Mrs. Jenkins hobbling down the aisle, struggling under the weight of her bags. With a gentle smile, Janice hurried over. "Let me help you, ma'am," she said softly, taking the bags. Mrs. Jenkins beamed gratefully as Janice led her to a seat. Sitting together, Janice listened closely as the elderly woman spoke of her own regrets and sorrows. Something inside Janice warmed; she was helping ease another's burdens, just as Olivia had once done for her.

Mrs. Jenkins has been a long-time member of the congregation. She is a sweet and gentle soul, always wearing

117

a soft smile on her face. She has silver hair that she keeps neatly styled and wears simple dresses with floral patterns. Despite her age, Mrs. Jenkins is still active in the community and is known for her kindness and compassion. She has a comforting presence and often offers words of encouragement to those who need it. Janice was drawn to Mrs. Jenkins' warmth and saw helping her as an opportunity to give back and spread some joy.

As the service ended, Janice walked Mrs. Jenkins out. "You are so kind, dear," the woman said, patting Janice's cheek. Her smiling eyes held no judgment, only understanding. Janice bid her goodbye, feeling lighter as if a piece of the ache in her heart had lifted away. She left resolved to keep helping in small ways, bringing comfort through compassion just as her parents had taught. And somehow, doing good for others helped soothe Janice's own wounded soul. A glimmer of hope took root that, in time, she, too, might find redemption and healing.

Olivia walked the streets aimlessly, avoiding church, much to her parent's disappointment, still lost in a haze of sadness. Before long, her feet carried her to the neighborhood animal shelter. Inside, joyful barks and meows greeted her. She spoke to the manager, asking if she could see the animals in the back.

When she walked through the doors that separated the front of the animal shelter from the kennel section, a smile spread across Olivia's face. The first smile in a long time. She asked if she could stay a few minutes to play with some of the animals. The manager agreed, saying they were short on volunteers, so she could stay as long as she wanted. Olivia poured her heart into playing with the pets, brushing their soft fur, and refilling food and water. For a few blissful hours, she lost herself in caring for others and felt her troubled mind begin to settle.

As she cuddled a litter of newborn kittens, memories of Janice came flooding back. The unconditional love these animals gave mirrored the compassion Janice had shown her since they met. Guilt washed over Olivia as she realized how much she had taken her friend's kindness for granted all this time. A tiny ball of fur nudged her hand, snuggling close. Olivia stroked its head, tears threatening to spill over. She thought of all the times Janice had comforted her so simply, just by being present. Now, that light in her life was gone, and it was all her fault for the cruel words said in anger.

"I am so sorry," she whispered to the kitten, who blinked up at her with innocent eyes. Olivia knew that someday she must find a way to apologize properly to Janice, too. Until then, she would keep caring for helpless creatures to honor her friend's memory and heal her wounded heart. Olivia and Janice each found purpose in service to others as they grieved the loss of their friendship. Volunteering with pets and helping the elderly, they learned that nurturing life outside themselves could heal their wounded souls.

As the weeks passed, the girls found relief in quiet moments. After school, they immersed themselves in the Scriptures for guidance and comfort. Janice took strength from lessons of forgiveness, while Olivia found wisdom in passages about redemption. Janice read, "Bear with each other and forgive one another," Colossians 3:13. She thought of Livvy's kindness even after their fight. From that day, Janice prayed daily for a chance to make amends.

Similarly, a verse struck Olivia while flipping through the New Testament at home: Romans 12:18, "If it is possible, as far as it depends on you, live at peace with everyone." She wanted nothing more than to reconcile, yet fear held her back. But through service and prayer, the girls' hearts gradually mended. However, they had not spoken since a glimmer of understanding flowered between them.

In time, through compassion for others and seeking truth within, Olivia and Janice came to accept responsibility for the past. Their wounded hearts knew that with courage and faith, all things were possible, even the healing of their treasured friendship.

Olivia sat alone in her room, flipping through old photographs. Pictures of smiling family vacations and school events had once brought her joy but now only reminded her of what was missing.

Then, she came upon snapshots from happier days with Janice. There they were, eating cotton candy at the county fair, flushed and giggling. Olivia's heart ached with longing for that easiness between them. She lingered on her favorite, a selfie of them with arms around each other, captured after volunteering at the shelter. Joy, compassion, and purpose shone from their faces. At that moment, all the hurt seemed far away.

Olivia hugged the photo to her chest, hot tears spilling once more. All this time spent apart had only reinforced what she had known from the beginning, that Janice was her truest companion, who calmed the tumult in her soul. A steely determination took hold. She was done hiding from the past and had come to terms with her guilt. All that remained was to take the chance of making things right again. With trembling hands, Olivia pulled out paper and pen, ready at last to reach across the chasm between them. This time, she would send the olive branch, come what may.

After writing and signing the letter, Olivia walked to the mailbox with renewed courage, letter in hand. As she slipped it inside, she sent up a prayer that Janice would accept her apology. Only time would tell if their bond could be mended.

Days passed with no word from Janice, hope wavering. But Olivia remained resolute, finding solace in service and Scripture. She chose to meet difficulty with patience and faith, as Janice had taught her.

Then, one morning, a knock sounded at the door. Olivia flew down the stairs and threw it open, breath catching at the visitor standing nervously outside.

"Janice," she whispered. Eyes brimming, the girls stood regarding each other, a chasm of experiences between them. Yet underneath, their souls recognized a kindred spirit. At that moment, all that needed to be said was unspoken. They fell into each other's arms and wept tears of release, and hurt drifted away on the breeze. Though cracks remained, the foundation of care they had built was sturdier than before.

They spent the day talking through all that had happened, truly listening without judgment. In time and forgiveness, understanding dawned; through struggle, they had each found inner strength, compassion, and wisdom that the other lacked alone. Most importantly, their friendship had endured. As sunset fell, Olivia walked Janice home with Heartlight once more. Through acceptance and empathy, their bond was rekindled anew, forged deeper by experiences, and ready to rediscover its beauty. Their faith in each other and life's capacity for hope had been restored.

CHAPTER 11
COMING TOGETHER

Olivia sat quietly in the pew, lost in thought as Pastor Thomas delivered the sermon. It had been a week since she and Janice reconciled, but their friendship still felt tentative. She was relieved and grateful that they had reconciled; however, it had been a tough week without her, and Olivia missed their conversations and shared experiences.

There was still a tiny part of Olivia that was worried about their friendship. She had hoped that their reconciliation was not just a temporary fix and that they could truly move forward and rebuild their bond. She was cautiously hopeful but also a little nervous about what the future held for the friendship.

Olivia missed Janice's comforting presence beside her in church. As she gazed up at the large glass windows, a flash of yellow entered her periphery. Olivia turned and saw Janice approaching hesitantly from the back of the church.

Their eyes met, and Janice offered a small, hopeful smile.

Olivia smiled back, feeling a warmth spread through her chest. She scooted over to make room, and Janice slipped into the pew next to her. They sat in silence, listening as Pastor Thomas spoke of mercy and forgiveness. When their fingers brushed tentatively, Olivia took Janice's hand in hers, and Janice squeezed it gently. They said nothing, simply drinking in the solace of each other's company once more. A calm understanding passed between them.

After the service, Olivia walked Janice out. "I am glad you came," she said softly.

Janice nodded. "Me too. I have missed you, Liv."

Olivia swallowed the lump in her throat. "I have missed you too." A breeze rustled the tree branches above them.

Janice met Olivia's gaze steadily. "Do you maybe want to get lunch together? We could talk if you would like."

Olivia felt herself relax. "I would like that."

Janice was overjoyed. It meant so much to her that Olivia wanted to spend more time together, especially after everything they had been through. It made Janice feel valued and accepted. She knew their bond was strong, but Olivia's invitation reinforced that and gave Janice a sense of belonging. She was excited to share a meal and continue their conversations. It was a moment of hope and connection for both.

They smiled at each other, hands still clasped loosely between them. Through small acts of compassion, their friendship was taking its first tentative steps toward healing. At the café, Olivia drank her milkshake silently while Janice toyed with her sandwich. "I owe you an apology," Olivia said finally, playing with her coaster.

Janice looked up, eyes soft. "You don't have to–"

"Yes, I do." Olivia took a shaky breath. "What I said, how I acted, it was unforgivable. All this time, you were the only thing keeping me afloat, and I threw that back into your face. You were hurting, and I kicked you while you were down." Tears slipped down Olivia's cheeks, but she smiled through them. "You have to know how sorry I am. Whatever you need from me, it is yours. I just hope that someday, you can find it in your heart to forgive me."

Janice reached over, brushing Olivia's tears away, "There is nothing to forgive. We both said things, but being apart only made me realize you are my best friend."

Olivia grinned. "I wouldn't trade you for anything." A sob of relief escaped Olivia as she squeezed Janice tight. "I will spend the rest of my life making it up to you, I promise."

Janice laughed softly. "Just being with you is enough." They smiled at each other through happy tears, their bond reaffirmed and strong as ever.

Olivia sipped her chocolate milkshake as color returned to Janice's cheeks. "It was awful without you," she admitted. "I kept replaying what happened, wishing I could take it all back."

Janice stared into her strawberry shake. "Me too. The days felt so long and empty. All I wanted was to hear your laugh again." A small smile broke through. "Remember how we used to joke that our souls were stitched together? Being apart just made me realize how true that really is."

Nodding, Olivia covered Janice's hand with her own. "I felt lost without you, my anchor. You are the only one who really understands me." She sighed. "I know we hurt each other, but I also know that whatever comes, we are stronger facing it together."

"You are right." Janice's smile grew more confident. "Nothing could ever change how much you mean to me. You are my best friend."

Warmth bloomed in Olivia's chest to see hope shining in Janice's eyes once more. After so much turmoil, sitting there in this bubble of quiet contentment was a comfort. Their bond was healing, and in time, she believed their friendship would grow even deeper to withstand this trial. For now, savoring the simple joy of Janice's presence at her side was enough.

At school, rumors swirled about Olivia and Janice making up. People whispered about them in the halls, questioning what their reconciliation meant and whether it would last. Janice tried not to let it get to her as she switched books in her locker. She had Olivia back, and that was all that mattered.

Still, when a girl snickered, "You two are so dramatic," Janice could not help shooting a sharp look. She did her best to ignore the stares and muttered comments during History. Instead, she focused on envisioning her plans with Olivia that weekend, a small smile playing on her lips.

By the end of the day, they met at their usual bench with happy relief. Olivia looped her arm through Janice's as they walked. "Ready to get out of here?" she asked brightly.

Janice laughed. "More than ready. I swear people were talking about us non-stop."

Olivia squeezed her arm. "Don't pay them any mind. We have each other."

With that reassurance, their chatter and gossip seemed to fade into the background. All that existed was the warm comfort of their friendship, repaired and blossoming once more. As they walked to Olivia's house, Janice's steps felt lighter than they had in weeks.

"Being apart taught me a lot," she reflected. "Like how much I take you for granted. And that nothing is more important than the people you care about."

Olivia sighed. "I should have been more understanding instead of getting so angry. You were there for me through everything, and I was not there when you needed me most."

"No more than I was for you," Janice reminded gently. "We both messed up. But I think... being apart showed me to focus on compassion instead of pride." She met Olivia's eyes. "And that no matter what, you are my family. That will never change."

A smile broke across Olivia's face at Janice's words. "You are so right. Getting a second chance to be with you has made me appreciate you and our friendship even more."

She threw an arm around Janice's shoulders. "From now on, I vow to have more patience too." Their laughter drifted on the breeze, lighthearted once more now that understanding had taken root. The hard lessons of their separation were fading, leaving behind deeper love and care for one another.

Olivia invited Janice to her home to watch a movie. Janice felt a mix of excitement and nervousness. It was such a kind gesture and showed that she truly valued their friendship. However, being invited into her home, which was so different from Janice's, made her a bit self-conscious.

She was worried about fitting in and not wanting to

feel like an outsider. But despite those insecurities, Janice was grateful for the opportunity to spend more time with Olivia and get to know her better. It was a step towards deepening their friendship, and Janice was really looking forward to going.

Unbeknownst to Janice, Olivia discussed inviting Janice to her home with her parents. At first, her parents were a bit hesitant. They expressed some concerns about their differences in backgrounds and whether it would be appropriate for the girls to spend time together outside of church. But after the conversation, explaining how much Janice means to Olivia and how their friendship has helped both of them grow, they agreed to let her come over. They were open-minded and understood the importance of embracing diversity and building meaningful connections.

Olivia passed Janice the popcorn as they settled under a blanket to watch The Princess Bride. "I still can't believe we let something like an argument come between us, even for a little while," she mused.

Janice leaned onto her shoulder. "Me either. There are probably still things we need to work on, you know? Old wounds do not just disappear."

Nodding slowly, Olivia threaded her fingers through Janice's. "But we will face them together this time. Our friendship... it feels different now. Deeper, somehow."

"Like we have come out the other side of a storm and are all the stronger for surviving it," Janice agreed softly. "Things will never be quite the same, but that is not a bad thing. It means we will appreciate every moment together even more."

Olivia smiled, pressing a kiss to Janice's hair as Westley and Buttercup bantered on screen. "You always know just what to say. I am lucky to have you."

A peaceful contentment hummed between them. Though cracks remained, mending was a lifelong journey, and they now walked hand in hand. Their bond had endured, emerging tempered by truth, understanding, and a love neither time nor trials could weaken. They enjoyed the rest of the movie in silence, holding hands and smiling.

The next day, after school, they met at their bench in the playground. Janice kept glancing at Olivia with an unreadable smile. "You are being weird," Olivia chuckled. "What is on your mind?"

Janice laughed, linking their arms. "I was thinking we should get matching friendship bracelets. You know, to symbolize how strong our bond is."

Warmth bloomed in Olivia's chest. "I love that idea, Jan!" She squeezed Janice's hand. "Let's go right now; I don't want to wait another moment."

The jewelry store was a small, locally owned boutique with a charming display of delicate and meaningful pieces. The store had a warm and inviting atmosphere, with soft lighting and a friendly salesperson who took the time to help Olivia and Janice find the perfect bracelets. They decided to split the cost of the bracelets as a symbol of their shared commitment to the friendship.

It was important for both to contribute equally and show their bond was built on mutual respect and support. They wanted the friendship bracelets to represent unity and to remind them of the special connection they have. It was a special moment, selecting those bracelets together and exchanging them as a symbol of their enduring friendship.

At the jeweler, they debated designs with gleeful enthusiasm. In the end, they chose thin silver chains dotted with purple stones, their favorite color. The bracelets fit snugly on their wrists, shining symbols of their sisterhood. Olivia admired the way their bracelets tangled together, beaming at Janice. "This is perfect. A reminder every day of the unbreakable bond we share, no matter what's to come."

Janice's eyes shone with joyful tears as she hugged Olivia closely. "You will always be my family. I am so glad we will wear these with pride."

Their bracelets chimed softly in the breeze, outward symbols of a love that ran far deeper. Olivia met her eyes with a soft smile. "Me too. Every effort was worth it to have you back by my side. Our friendship will always be the most important thing."

"Milkshake time?" Olivia asked, smiling.

"Absolutely," Janice responded gleefully.

Janice raised her glass in a toast. "To us, and the unbreakable bond we share." Olivia's glass chimed lightly against hers. She looked at Janice with tender affection, so thankful their love proved strong enough to withstand any storm. As they sat chatting joyfully, any lingering shadows from their rift seemed to fade completely. The hard journey of reconciliation was now a distant memory, left behind in place of renewed understanding and a sisterhood deeper than ever before.

Their matching bracelets glimmered in the sunset on their walk home, outward signs of an unshakable connection that would endure whatever trials the future held.

CHAPTER 12
LIGHT IN DARK TIMES

Janice was jolted awake by the shrill ringing of her phone. She rolled over groggily and glanced at the clock; it was just past midnight. Her heart sank as she saw her neighbor Betty's number on the call display. "Betty, it is late. Is everything okay?" Janice answered nervously.

"Janice dear, I'm so sorry to wake you," Betty said, her voice trembling. "But it's your grandmother... she collapsed as she was getting ready for bed. An ambulance just took her to Mercy Hospital."

Betty is Janice's grandmother's dearest friend. She has been a source of support for her grandmother over the years, especially during difficult times. They have known each other for a long time and have a close bond. When her grandmother needed someone to lean on, she went to Betty's house for comfort and companionship.

Janice felt the blood drain from her face. Her grandmother was the only family she had left. "Is she... is she..." Janice could not bring herself to say the words.

"We don't know anything for certain yet," Betty said gently. "But it did not look good, Janice. You better get to the hospital right away."

Janice threw on some clothes and raced to her phone to call a taxi, her mind spinning. Her grandmother just had to be okay; Janice didn't know how she could go on without her. As the cab sped through the dark, empty streets, Janice felt strangely calm despite the turmoil inside.

She knew who she needed: Olivia.

Janice pulled out her phone with shaky hands and called Olivia from the cab through tears. Olivia answered instantly, and Janice explained what happened between sobs.

"Olivia... I am so scared. Will… will you come to the hospital with me? I do not think I can do this alone." To her relief, Olivia said she would ask her father to drive her to meet Janice right away. Olivia's father understood the gravity of the situation and wanted to support her in any way he could. Despite any previous concerns he may have had about her friendship with Janice, he was there for when Olivia needed him most. It was a moment that strengthened their bond as father and daughter.

As Janice arrived at Mercy Hospital, she saw Olivia and her father near the entrance. Olivia enveloped Janice in a tight hug as they walked inside, not letting go of her hand. "I am here," Olivia whispered. "And I am not leaving your side. We will get through this together."

Janice gripped Olivia's hand tightly, feeling steadied by her friend's loving presence. They made their way to the ICU, bracing themselves for what lay ahead. Janice anxiously paced the cramped waiting room as Olivia and her father watched helplessly from their chairs. Olivia's father understood the importance of being there with her and providing support during this difficult time. They sat together, waiting for updates and offering each other comfort. His presence meant a lot to both girls, and they were grateful to have him by their sides.

When a weary doctor finally emerged, Janice froze, not wanting to hear the news but needing to know. "Miss Thompson?" the doctor said gently. "Your grandmother had a severe heart attack. We have done all we can, but I am afraid her heart is very weakened, and her other organs are starting to shut down. Her condition is critical." Janice opened her mouth, but no words came out. She felt Olivia take her hand and squeeze it tightly.

"What are her chances?" Olivia asked bravely.

The doctor sighed. "It is hard to say definitively. She is a fighter, but the next 24 hours will be crucial. We are doing everything in our power to stabilize her, but you need to prepare yourselves for any outcome."

Tears slid silently down Janice's face. *How could this be happening?* Grammy was all she had left. Janice could not picture her world without her grandmother's warm smile and embrace. She began trembling uncontrollably as the reality of the situation hit her. Olivia wrapped Janice in a hug as her body shook with helpless sobs.

All Janice could do now was pray for a miracle. Janice sobbed into Olivia's shoulder, her body racked with grief. Olivia held her close, gently rubbing her back in comfort. Though tears stung her own eyes at the thought of losing Ruth, Olivia willed herself to remain strong for Janice's sake.

"I've got you," Olivia whispered. "Let it all out. I am here." Her heart swelled with love for her dearest friend, who had endured so much suffering yet remained so selflessly kind. At that moment, Olivia vowed silently to do everything she could to ease Janice's anguish.

Once Janice's tears subsided into quiet hiccups, Olivia led her to the plastic waiting room chairs, where Olivia's father was waiting. He could tell Janice had received unwelcome news. He gently offered his support, for which Janice was grateful. Olivia sat beside Janice, their arms intertwined, and pulled some tissues from her pocket to dry Janice's flushed cheeks.

Though words seemed insufficient, Olivia offered what little solace she could. "She is a fighter. She loves you so much; I know that gives her strength."

Janice nodded wearily, leaning into the comfort of Olivia's embrace as fresh tears fell. Looking upon her grief-stricken face, Olivia's own tears threatened to overflow at the enormity of Janice's sorrow. Still, she reminded herself that Janice needed her strength now more than ever. Olivia would be her rock, as Janice had been for her through so many trials.

Their bond would see them through this darkest of nights. Janice stared blankly at the ICU doors, waiting and hoping desperately for any news. As hours crept by with her grandmother's status unchanged, Janice was finding it harder to hold on to hope.

"What if she... does not make it?" Janice whispered, a fresh wave of tears spilling over. "I do not know what I will do without her, Olivia."

"Oh, Janice! I wish I knew what to say," Olivia replied sadly, pulling her into another embrace. "All I know is that your grandmother raised an amazing woman, and she would want you to keep living bravely, just as she taught you." Janice nodded, taking a deep, shaky breath. She knew Olivia was right. Grammy had always believed in the power of prayer. Right now, Janice wanted and needed to believe, too.

"Olivia, will you pray with me?"

"Of course."

They joined hands over Janice's lap and bowed their heads. Olivia spoke words of comfort as Janice silently pleaded for Ruth's recovery.

"Please, God," she prayed. "Please do not take her from me too. I will do anything; be stronger; just do not let her die."

Olivia's father added, "God, grant us the serenity to accept the things we cannot change, courage to change the things we can, and wisdom to know the difference."

It was a prayer that both girls appreciated, especially Janice.

A sense of calm washed over Janice as Olivia's and her father's kind words and their entwined hands anchored her. Her faith, long tested, was holding on through the depths of darkness. And Janice knew that even if the worst came to pass, she would continue with Olivia by her side.

As the first rays of dawn filtered through the windows, the doctor re-emerged. Janice and Olivia stood on shaking legs, clinging to each other in anticipation of whatever news was to come. "Miss Thompson," the doctor said gently. "I have an update on your grandmother's condition."

Janice held her breath, Olivia squeezing her hand in support. "Your grandmother made it through the night. Her vitals have stabilized, and we have managed to get her heart under better control for now. She is not out of the woods yet, but this is a very good sign."

Janice's knees buckled in relief and gratitude. Olivia caught her elbow just in time, clinging to her friend as grateful sobs racked her body once more.

"She is still unconscious, but you can go sit with her now if you would like," the doctor continued softly. Janice nodded through her tears. With Olivia's help, she steadied herself to see her grandmother. Though unconscious, her grandmother seemed peaceful at last. Janice brought Grammy's limp hand to her cheek, kissing it softly.

"Thank you, God, for not taking her from me," she whispered. Her faith, tested to its limits, had prevailed through the crisis. Now Janice could allow herself to collapse, exhausted but hopeful, into Olivia's waiting arms. Mary would live to see another day, and for that, Janice was eternally grateful.

Over the following days, Olivia remained by Janice's side steadfastly. When Janice was too exhausted to cook, Olivia brought meals from her mother's kitchen, and Olivia's dad drove her to and from the hospital without complaint. Though her grandmother's condition gradually improved, every ache or IV adjustment induced fresh waves of panic in Janice. But Olivia was always there with a comforting hand on Janice's back or kind words of reassurance. She helped Janice research heart conditions on the Internet and asked knowledgeable questions of the doctors.

In quieter moments, Olivia simply kept Janice company in the hospital room, knowing her presence offered its own calm reassurance. As Janice drifted in and out of an anxious doze, Olivia read or sketched nearby, awake to fetch nurses at any change. The nursing staff began to see Olivia as part of the family, too.

"Your sister is quite devoted to you both," one remarked to Janice. Janice smiled wanly. "Sister" did not quite cover the multitudes of what Olivia meant to her. She did not know what she would do without Olivia's loyal, loving care through this trial.

Each slight improvement in her grandmother lifted Janice's spirits a little more. But through it all, the most steadying force was Olivia, who selflessly gave of herself to hold Janice together with unwavering gentleness and love.

Janice held her grandmother's frail hand, lightly running her thumb over sunspot-freckled skin. Though weak, Ruth recognized her touch even in her half-conscious state.

Outside, dusk fell over a world Janice barely noticed these days. "Grandma, it is me," Janice whispered. "I am here, just like always. You have taught me that nothing lasts, not even life..." Her voice trembled. "But please, Gram, not your life. Not yet." Janice told her of each small triumph, a smile at Olivia's joke, steady beeps on the heart monitor greeting each dawn. "You have lived through so much," she said. "You can't leave me now. I need you. I will work harder and be better if you just keep breathing."

Tears wet her grandmother's blanket as Janice begged a higher power for lenience. "Just a little longer," she pleaded. "I promise I will never waste a day. But Gram, I cannot do this without you."

At the door, Olivia's sad eyes met Janice's red-rimmed ones. She knew no words could soothe this agony or replace the space a grandmother occupies in a granddaughter's soul. All she could offer was her steadying presence, praying Janice would not be made to bury yet another loved one. For now, that would have to be enough.

Janice pressed a final kiss to her grandmother's cheek. "Please," she whispered. "Fight for me." Janice closed her eyes as tears streamed down her face. The delicate rise and fall of her grandmother's chest were her only comfort. She did not know how much longer she could endure this purgatory of waiting and fear.

A gentle hand squeezed her shoulder. "Come with me and rest, Janice. I'll sit with you," said Olivia softly. Though reluctant, Janice knew her strength was fading. She pressed a final kiss to Mary's hand before allowing Olivia to lead her away.

In the empty hospital hall, Janice broke down in Olivia's embrace. "I can't lose her too, Liv. She is all I have left."

"I know, darling," whispered Olivia, stroking her hair. "But have faith; your grandmother is the strongest woman I know. And I am here for you, always." Janice took comfort in Olivia's unwavering presence, the sole fixed point as her world hung in precarious balance.

Exhausted but finding peace in Olivia's embrace, Janice clung to the hope that her grandmother would pull through. She had survived this long through resilience and faith; Olivia's loyalty gave Janice strength to believe those virtues could see her through the crisis. For now, that would have to be enough.

CHAPTER 13
GROWTH AND GRATITUDE

Janice held her grandmother's hand tightly, praying in silence as the steady beep of machines filled the room. Olivia stood close by in support, her eyes fixed on Ruth's pale face. Then, Janice felt a weak squeeze as Janice's grandmother's eyes were slowly opening.

"Gramma?" Janice whispered in disbelief. Ruth smiled faintly at the sight of Janice, bringing tears of joy to her eyes. "Oh, Gramma, I knew you would come back to me!"

Overcome with relief, Janice embraced her grandmother gently. Olivia sighed thankfully, sending prayers of gratitude. The doctor was summoned and was delighted to see Ruth awake.

Dr. Patel was an incredible woman with a warm smile and kind eyes. She had a calming presence that instantly made you feel at ease. She is an experienced physician in cardiology who genuinely cares about her patients. She took the time to explain everything to Janice, answered all her questions, and provided a sense of hope.

After Dr. Patel examined Ruth vitals, she declared her out of danger, much to the elation of Janice and Olivia. Janice admitted she would forever be grateful to her for giving her the good news about her grandmother's health.

In the following days, Ruth steadily recovered thanks to the doctors and nurses' round-the-clock care and Janice's unwavering devotion. Though weak, she felt blessed by life and insisted Janice continue pursuing her dreams. But Janice was resolved to remain by her grandmother's side, aided by Olivia in caring for her needs. She soon noticed the bond between the girls and encouraged them to experience youth together.

Janice smiled when her grandmother said they should "experience youth." This was something she said often to Janice over the past few years.

Ruth would often plan little adventures for Janice, like picnics in the park or taking her to cultural events in the city. She believed in the importance of exploring new places, trying new things, and appreciating the beauty of the world around us. She encouraged Janice to follow her passions and pursue her dreams. Whether it was supporting Janice's love for writing or cheering on her artistic endeavors, she believed in the power of self-expression and personal growth.

Janice's grandmother taught her the value of cherishing the present and finding happiness in the simplest of moments. Ruth reminded her to laugh, play, and be grateful for the blessings in her life. Her love and encouragement have been instrumental in shaping Janice's youth and fostering their deep bond. Janice will forever be grateful to her for the love and guidance she has given her.

Witnessing Ruth's zest for life further kindled Janice's faith in defying the odds. She realized the purpose of cherishing each moment and empowering others, as her grandmother had taught her. Olivia, too, found purpose in their restored hope and resilience against all troubles. Together, they gave thanks.

In the following weeks, Ruth showed steady improvement, though the doctors wished to keep her under observation. Janice visited daily, heartened by her Gramma's regaining strength and humor.

"You give me life, child," Ruth said, smiling. Janice tearfully kissed her hand, thankful for each precious moment. Despite fatigue, her grandmother insisted that Janice focus on school and friends, especially Olivia, whose company she enjoyed. Weary but determined, Janice found support in Olivia's love.

"She is like the mother I lost," Janice confessed one day in the hospital chapel. Olivia embraced her friend, sharing in her joy and sorrows. Through prayer and each other's comfort, their bond grew deeper. They both felt the need for some guidance and solace, so they decided to say a prayer together. It was a quiet moment of vulnerability and support.

The prayer they said was heartfelt, asking for strength, healing, and peace. They prayed for their loved ones, for Janice's grandmother's recovery, and for guidance to navigate the challenges Janice and Olivia were facing. Olivia's voice trembled a little as she spoke the words, but her sincerity brought tears to Janice's eyes. It was a beautiful moment of connection and shared faith as they both sought comfort and reassurance. They also asked for the strength to overcome their doubts and fears and for the wisdom to make the right choices in their lives. They also prayed for love and compassion to persevere through difficult times, both for themselves and others.

It was a simple prayer, but it carried the weight of their hopes and dreams and their deep desire to stay true to their friendship and the values they hold dear. In that chapel, Janice and Olivia found comfort, support, and a renewed sense of purpose.

After each Sunday service, Olivia would join Janice in bringing Ruth small gifts of cheer from the outdoors. Seeing her grandmother's delight uplifted Janice's spirit.

"You girls give me so much happiness. I feel blessed beyond words," she said with emotion. Together, the three of them drew strength as Janice's grandmother kept improving, her indomitable fire for life rekindled through their devotion.

When school resumed on Monday, so did the under-breath comments. During lunch in the cafeteria, Olivia noticed two girls smirking and muttering under their breaths about Janice. Olivia recognized one of the girls, Jessica. Fury swept through her at their cruelty. She marched over and stared them down.

"I have had enough of your bullying. Janice is ten times the person you will ever be," Olivia said coldly. The girls sneered, but Olivia stood her ground, recalling Janice's unwavering spirit in dark times. "You will leave her alone, or you will have to answer to me," she warned.

Word soon spread of Olivia's facing down Jessica and her friends. Students looked at Olivia in a new light, seeing her defend Janice so boldly. She no longer cared what others thought, only standing up for justice and her dear friend.

That evening, Olivia shyly confessed the confrontation to Janice. "You didn't have to do that," Janice said in admiration.

"But I wanted to, like you always, stand up for me," Olivia smiled. Janice gazed at her friend proudly, seeing the strong woman she was becoming thanks to their bond of empathy, courage, and love.

That Sunday, following a near eventless week at school, Olivia, with her family, was listening intently during a guest sermon on compassion. She had grown comfortable with uncertainty, respecting faith as a personal journey. The visiting pastor had been here several times in the past.

Pastor Jameson was a tall man with greying hair and a kind smile. He had a warm and welcoming presence, and his sermons were filled with wisdom and grace. He had a calming voice that always managed to captivate the congregation. It was refreshing to hear his unique perspectives on faith and the importance of embracing compassion in our lives.

This Sunday, it seemed he was speaking directly to Olivia as he spoke passionately of embracing life's mysteries through love for others. Olivia nodded thoughtfully, drawing parallels between faith and her friendship with Janice, both of which nurtured her spirit. She smiled, envisioning Janice's approving smile.

Although attending without Janice, Olivia felt her presence. Her friend had taught her that independence need not mean isolation. As the service ended, Olivia said a silent prayer for Ruth's recovery and Janice's resilience and smiled, feeling content in her patient search and grateful for lessons in acceptance.

Walking home, Olivia told her parents that she wanted to go to 'their' bench and sit for a while. They knew she was talking about the bench where Olivia and Janice had their many conversations. As she sat alone, Olivia reflected on small acts of kindness. She understood faith as a wellspring of hope, demonstrated through empathy. Her heart overflowed with gratitude for Janice, mentor of life's beauty, found even amid shadows. Olivia's identity now embraced doubts and living fully in each moment, finding pathways of light through connection.

As she got up to leave, Olivia decided to stop by to see Janice on her way home.

Her walk was quite serene and peaceful. It was as if Olivia was noticing the sun for the first time as it cast a warm glow over the neighborhood. As she made her way through the familiar streets, with a spring in her steps, she noticed the leaves rustling in the gentle breeze, creating a soothing sound. The scent of freshly cut grass and blooming flowers filled the air, adding a touch of nature's beauty to the scene. Along the way, she passed by houses, each with their own unique charm. Some had beautifully manicured gardens, while others had children playing in their yards. The neighborhood seemed to come alive with the sounds of laughter and the occasional sound of a lawnmower humming in the distance.

As she approached Janice's house, she noticed the comfortable little porch where they often sat and talked, especially since Ruth had been in the hospital. The paint on the house was slightly faded, but it exuded a warm and welcoming atmosphere. Janice's grandmother had planted colorful flowers near the entrance, adding a touch of vibrancy to the surroundings.

Olivia's walk to Janice's house was a peaceful and comforting experience, offering a glimpse into the everyday beauty of both neighborhoods and the sense of community that seemed alive.

Janice opened the door, and her face was glowing with joyous news, "Gramma is coming home!" she beamed. Olivia gasped happily and embraced her friend. Janice's eyes shone with tears and merriment. "The doctors say with rest, she will continue gaining strength at home." Relief swept over Olivia as she shed tears of joy with Janice. Dark clouds of fear and grief now scattered from Janice's mind in rays of hope. She gazed upon Olivia, her heart overflowing. "Livvy, I cannot thank you enough for standing with me through this trial. Your devotion means more than I can say." Olivia clasped Janice's hands warmly.

"There is no place I would rather be than at your side through every sunrise and sunset. You both brought so much light to my world." Their smiles reflected the radiance of joyful days ahead, of healing hearts and an unbreakable bond forging their spirits ever stronger. They decided to have a celebratory milkshake at the diner.

Olivia and Janice nestled into a booth, drinks in hand. For some time, they simply savored this moment of quietude after tumult. Janice sighed contentedly.

"I never thought I would see Gramma laugh again after her heart attack. But your faith in her kept mine burning, too." Janice said as she squeezed her friend's hand warmly.

"I was so scared of losing the only family you have left. You faced it all with pure courage and grace. I admire you beyond words."

157

Janice's eyes glistened. "Your strength and friendship gave me much-needed strength during this ordeal. We have endured this test together. Through it, I believe our bond has flowered into something truly beautiful." Olivia nodded, whispering a prayer of thanks.

Lifting her glass in a toast, Janice's eyes danced. "To family we choose, and whose blood ties us, to the light found in each soul we touch along the way."

At that moment, Olivia saw their friendship bracelets on their wrists. Her thoughts were filled with a mix of appreciation and joy. Seeing the bracelets reminded her of the journey she and Janice had been on together, the challenges they had faced, and the strengthened bond they now shared. They symbolized not only their deepening friendship but also the support and understanding they had provided each other throughout their struggles. They served as a tangible reminder of the deep connection they had formed and the growth they had experienced together.

At that moment, Olivia felt a profound sense of gratitude for Janice's presence in her life. The bracelets represented a symbol of trust, compassion, and resilience, a constant reminder of the strength and beauty that can emerge from even the most unlikely friendships. Seeing both bracelets on their wrists brought a sense of warmth, comfort, and a renewed commitment to their friendship. It was a heartwarming reminder of the power of connection and the importance of knowing that someone is always there for you.

Janice noticed Olivia looking at their bracelets. "These bracelets represent so much more than just a simple accessory," Janice said. "To me, they symbolize the bond we have formed, the ups and downs we have faced together, and the support we' have given each other." Seeing those bracelets reminded Janice of the deep connection they have been sharing and how far they have come since they first met.

"These are a constant reminder of the strength and resilience we have, and it reassures me that no matter what challenges come our way, we will always have each other's backs."

Olivia stared with her mouth open. "That is exactly what I have been thinking!" They shared a loud laugh, causing other patrons to turn their heads. But the girls did not care; they had each other, and that is all that mattered.

Another chapter of love and resilience was theirs.

Leaving the diner, they walked straight to their bench. Watching the sunset, Janice sighed contentedly. "Such adventures lie ahead, Livvy, for souls as bright as yours."

Olivia smiled, gazing at scattered colors. "I never dreamed I would find my calling through friendship's light." Janice took her hand warmly. "Our bond has taught empathy and courage."

Olivia's eyes gleamed with the mysteries of tomorrow. "Gramma will heal fully thanks to your care, as I have through your love and wisdom. Our journeys will continue to blossom, sunk deep in understanding."

Janice leaned her head on Olivia's shoulder, dazzled by destiny's design. "However far our paths wind, sisters of the soul, we will remain. Our friendship has shaped not just who we are but who we will become for all we touch." In each other's eyes, worlds of promise shone. They embraced tenderly as they each started their walk home.

Janice smiled through misting eyes; palms clasped around Olivia's as she repeated a phrase the pastor said during the service, "Though challenges await, your friendship anchors me ever strong in faith that goodness prevails through empathy shown."

Gazing deep at one another, worlds of promise glimmered. They lingered there silently, needing no further words to express souls woven in sacred trust. Janice's eyes shone with gratitude for such a gift.

Parting with a final squeeze, Olivia watched Janice walk away. A prayer slipped from her heart for Janice's continued resilience and Gramma's full recovery. Most of all, she thanked God for bringing such a soul into her life to illuminate her journey, come what may. Her steps turned homeward through deepening dusk, her soul overflowing with affection and hope for all the wonders their bond would yet withstand.

CHAPTER 14
FAREWELLS AND HELLOS

Olivia sat on her porch swing, gazing out at the sprawling summer sky. Warm breezes rustled the oak leaves as she anticipated Janice's arrival. Their freshman year of high school loomed ahead like a shimmering horizon filled with promise and adventure. A clamor of footsteps echoed down the street, and Janice appeared, beaming brighter than the morning sun.

"It is finally here!" she exclaimed, breathless. Olivia grinned. "Summer at last. Think of all the possibilities..."

Taking a seat, Janice sighed contentedly. "It seems like only yesterday we met, yet so much has changed. I never knew I could feel this happy." Olivia squeezed her hand. "We have endured so much together. I still remember that chance hot chocolate spill like it was yesterday." Chuckling, Janice replied, "Funny how small moments can lead to the greatest things."

As they brainstormed summer plans, Olivia noticed Janice seemed distracted. "What's troubling you?"

Janice shrugged. "Just imagining what's next after summer ends. High school...what if we grow apart?"

Olivia embraced her reassuringly. "Nothing could ever separate us. We'll face whatever comes, side by side." Gazing at their friendship bracelets, Janice smiled. "You always know how to cheer me up. I am going to cherish every day of freedom!"

Their laughter echoed across the lawn. Though unsure paths lay ahead, their bond would always guide them home. Janice grinned, recounting the past school year. "Remember when I aced that math test? And you winning the essay contest; I am so proud!"

Olivia squeezed her hand. "And I could never have volunteered at the shelter without your inspiration. We make such a great team."

Just then, Ruth appeared on the sidewalk. Walking up to Olivia's porch, beaming, she said, "Look at my girls, all grown up! I am so blessed to see the women you have become. Making room on the swing, Olivia insisted, "Come join us! We were just reminiscing on the year."

Ruth took a seat with a weary sigh, but her eyes shone with pride. "I remember Janice's first day of kindergarten like it was yesterday. And now high school! Where does the time go?" Janice wrapped her arm around her.

"I will always be your little girl. But it helps to have Liv by my side every step."

Her grandmother nodded approvingly. "I am grateful every day for the happiness you have brought each other. Now, what are your summer plans? I want to hear it all!" As the girls chattered excitedly, Ruth watched on with a smile, content seeing her family as a whole and hopeful for their bright futures blossoming ahead.

That evening, at Janice's house, the girls helped Ruth prepare a feast fit for queens. Olivia arrived with dishes in tow. Not surprisingly, Olivia's parents and brother also entered, bearing flowers.

"We are so happy to celebrate with all of you," Olivia's mom said warmly. Grinning, Janice almost tackled

Olivia with a big hug, "You made it!" As the table filled with mouthwatering scents, Janice squeezed her grandmother's hands. "Thank you for being well enough to do this. I am the lucky one." Ruth kissed her forehead affectionately. "I would not miss it for the world. Now, let's eat!"

Olivia was mixed with emotions when her parents agreed to go with her to Janice's house. On the one hand, she was glad they were there to share in the joy and witness the bond that she and Janice had forged. Their presence showed support and acceptance of their friendship. On the other hand, Olivia could not help but feel a bit anxious. She knew her parents had worried about Janice being a bad influence on her in the past, and there were moments of tension between them due to their different backgrounds. Olivia wanted everything to go perfectly, to prove to her parents that Janice was a genuinely good person and their friendship was worth celebrating.

But in the end, their presence brought a sense of unity and reconciliation. It gave her hope that maybe, just maybe, they were starting to understand the depth of their connection and see the positive influence Janice had on her life. It was a special moment for all of them, a small step towards bridging the gap between two different worlds.

Around the table, laughter and memories flowed freely. Olivia's parents shared stories about her growing up, much to the embarrassment of Olivia. They talked about how she was always curious and asking questions about everything, much like today, and how she loved to read and learn new things. They also mentioned how she always had a strong sense of empathy and a desire to help others. Even in her embarrassment, Olivia thought it was sweet of them to share those stories, and it was a great way for Janice and her grandmother to get to know me better.

Olivia glowed seeing her two families joined in harmony. She met Janice's gaze, and they smiled knowingly; after all they had endured, a simple joy like this was richest of all.

Later, as Olivia helped clear dishes, Janice caught her smile. "What is it?" Olivia nodded toward their blended families.

"All that really matters is right here; love has a way of making any place feel like home. You will always be part of my family."

While Olivia and Janice made their way to the front porch, Olivia's parents and brother remained inside, deep in conversation about nothing in particular with Ruth.

As they stargazed on the porch, Olivia finally found the courage to share her news. "I got accepted into my dream program," she said softly. "In Italy." Olivia had mixed feelings when telling Janice she would be going to school overseas. She was really excited about the opportunity to explore a new country and experience a different culture. Italy has always fascinated her, and she could not wait to see the historical sites, try the delicious food, and immerse herself in the beauty of the country.

However, Olivia also felt sad to be leaving Janice behind. They had become such good friends, and she knew she would miss her dearly and their conversations. She also did not want her to feel like she was abandoning her or that their friendship would not be the same when she returned. It was a bittersweet moment for Olivia, but she reassured Janice that their friendship meant everything to her and that she would be thinking of her while she was away.

Janice gasped in delight, then froze as the full meaning sunk in. "Livvy, that is amazing! I am so proud of you." She swallowed hard. "But... does this mean..."

"I leave next month." Olivia's voice trembled with emotion. "It's a once-in-a-lifetime chance, but the thought of being apart from you is unbearable."

Tears spilled down Janice's cheeks as she hugged Olivia closely. "Promise me we will keep in touch every day. Video chat, letters, everything."

"I promise." Olivia tightened her embrace, taking comfort in Janice's familiar warmth. "It will not be goodbye. Just see you later."

Janice had mixed feelings about what Olivia just told her. She was excited for Olivia because it was an amazing opportunity for her to explore a new country and have new experiences. But also, she felt a bit sad because she knew it would mean being apart from her for a while. They had been through so much together, and the thought of not having her by her side was a little daunting. But Janice also understood that this was a chance for her to grow and follow her dreams, so Janice knew she had to be supportive and remind herself that their friendship would always remain strong, no matter the distance.

There was a part of Janice that was afraid she might never see Olivia again. It is natural to have those worries, she thought, especially when someone you care about is going far away. But Janice also knew that true friendship could withstand distance and time apart. They had been through so many ups and downs, and she had faith that their bond would stay strong, no matter the miles between them. So, while there was a twinge of fear, she tried to focus on the positive, that they would always find their way back to each other, even if it took a little longer.

They stayed on the porch for quite some time, silent tears expressing what words could not. Though joy swelled in Olivia's heart, an equal ache emerged, leaving behind her true north. But Janice's loving support gave her relief, reminding them that no distance could diminish the bond they shared.

That summer was filled with so many memorable moments for the girls. They made sure to make the most of their time together. They went on so many adventures, exploring their town, trying out new cafes, and taking long walks in the park. They even had a mini road trip to the nearby beach, where they built sandcastles, laughed, and had deep conversations while watching the sunset. It was a summer of making beautiful memories and cherishing each other's company. They knew that Olivia's trip was on the horizon, so they wanted to create lasting memories to hold onto while they were apart.

The first part of summer flew by in a bittersweet blur of shared laughs and private tears. But at last, the morning dawned for Olivia's flight, and Janice insisted on seeing her off. Olivia's parents picked Janice up for the ride to the airport. Janice's grandmother approached Olivia with a warm smile. She expressed how grateful she was for her friendship with Janice and how much it meant to them both. She thanked Olivia for being a positive influence in Janice's life and for supporting her through tough times. Ruth also said she believed Olivia's trip to Italy would be an incredible opportunity for her to grow, explore, and learn. She encouraged Olivia to fully embrace the experience and bring back stories and memories to share with Janice when she returned.

Her words were so heartfelt and kind, and they made Olivia feel even more connected to Janice's family. It was a touching moment, and Olivia knew that despite the distance, their bond would remain strong.

At the airport, the many embraces were long, tearful, and lingering.

"I will call as soon as I land," Olivia promised in Janice's ear. Janice swallowed hard, fighting to keep her composure.

"And remember, this is not goodbye; it's see you later. Be safe, study hard, and let me know if you find any cute Italian guys!"

Olivia chuckled softly through her tears. "You had better have crazy adventures of your own to tell me about. I will be back before you know it."

A crackling announcement signaled it was time to board. With one final crushing hug, they clung to each other desperately, as if sheer force of will could halt the inevitable. Then, scrubbing her eyes, Janice waved bravely until Olivia vanished from sight. Her knees buckled, waves of grief crashing over her.

Once on the plane, Olivia pressed her palm against the window, longing to hold Janice close just a moment more. Then she steeled herself and walked resolutely towards the future, comforted by their unbreakable bond transcending all distance. Olivia typed a message to Janice with trembling fingers: *I miss you already. This is not goodbye; we will talk every day and video chat like our lives depend on it. I will be back before you know it, and nothing will ever separate us again. You are my soul sister for life. I love you endlessly.*

She pressed send, letting Janice's reply come when it may. Leaning back as the plane took off, Olivia gazed out at the endless sky, feeling both tiny and limitless all at once. A kaleidoscope of emotions swirled within: excitement, trepidation, grief. But strongest of all was the golden thread binding her irrevocably to Janice.

Though distance now divided their forms, their spirits would always be woven together. No trial could rupture that sacred bond. Olivia closed her eyes and visualized Janice's smile, drawing comfort until her phone dinged with a response. Janice: *I love you too, Liv. Have an amazing time, and follow your dreams. I will be right here, cheering you on every step. Our bond is unbreakable. Now, go conquer Italy!* 💜

Olivia smiled, relaxing in the unknown before her, safe in the knowledge that Janice, her soul's anchor, was only a call away. This was merely another phase of their odyssey. Their sisterly love had prevailed through every test thus far and would surely withstand whatever lay ahead.

Janice strode onto campus, taking a deep breath. A new start. She spotted a group laughing. Would they accept her? Then a thought, "You have got this." Olivia's words echoed in her mind, imbuing courage. Classes flew by in a whirl. Janice excelled but longed for Livvy's presence beside her. After a good video session filled with laughter and tears, resilience bloomed once more within.

Across the sea, Olivia navigated her new world with wonder and perseverance. Italy dawned on her like a strange dream, carrying scents of a home far from home. But each message from Janice brought sunlight and strength to endure.

Their correspondence flowed as naturally as conversation, binding them closer despite the physical void. Tales of triumphs, troubles, and everything between bridged the miles between. The sisterly bond held fast through challenges of the heart alone. As Janice conquered fears within new friendships, Olivia cultivated understandings beyond any book. Their spirits entwined nightly despite the distance, each dawn finding solace knowing the other walked in the parallel journey. Love lit their way across unknown paths, reunion always gleaming on the distant horizon.

That autumn, as the changing leaves heralded a new season, Olivia phoned Janice with news she was returning home for a visit.

When Olivia told Janice she was coming back from Italy for a visit, she was beyond excited! They had missed each other so much while Olivia was away and knew that she was making an effort to come back and see her meant the world. Janice felt a rush of joy and anticipation like they were going to have the chance to pick up where they left off and create new memories together. It was definitely a special feeling.

At the airport, Janice embraced her sister tightly. "You look happy and confident as the woman I always knew you would become."

Olivia smiled through tears. "And look at you, so strong and insightful. I am so proud of the woman you are blossoming into."

Holding hands, they walked out into the sunset to Olivia's father's car. Though bittersweet parting still loomed, for now, they savored reunion amid changing tides. Their bond remained solid as an oak, nurtured through trials into the grace that could weather any storm.

As they sat in Olivia's bedroom, reminiscing by flickering candlelight, reflections emerged of how far they had come since that fateful hot chocolate spill. Olivia shared stories with Janice about her trip to Italy. She told about the stunning architecture in cities like Rome and Florence and how she was awe-struck by the ancient ruins and grand cathedrals. She also described the vibrant atmosphere of the Italian markets, where she enjoyed sampling delicious street food and browsing through colorful stalls, tales of wandering through picturesque villages, indulging in gelato, and marveling at the breathtaking landscapes of Tuscany.

Olivia made sure to highlight the cultural experiences, too, like attending an opera performance and learning a few Italian phrases. Janice was really interested and excited to hear about Olivia's adventures, and Olivia loved sharing those moments with her.

Now, it was Janice's turn to share. She told her about the volunteer work she has been doing at the local soup kitchen and how it has been a really rewarding experience. Janice told Olivia that she had made new friends and had met some really cool people during Olivia's absence. One of her new friends is Sarah, who shares Janice's love for writing. They have been exchanging stories and poems, which has been a great way to express ourselves and bond over our shared passion.

Janice also talked about her high school. It is a typical suburban high school, bustling with students and a wide range of activities. There is a lot going on, from sports teams to clubs. It can get a bit overwhelming at times, but Janice tries to focus on her studies and stay involved in the activities that really matter to her, like volunteering and being there for my friends, and especially her grandmother.

Olivia asked Janice about her grandmother. "She has been such a pillar of strength for me," Janice said. She also told Olivia about the challenges they had been facing, especially with finances being tight. But despite all that,

Ruth continues to persevere with a smile on her face. She is such an incredible woman, and Janice admires her resilience. It is not always easy, and there are days when things feel overwhelming, but they have been managing. Ruth has been very supportive and understanding, and Janice expressed how grateful she is to have her grandmother by her side.

"I believe that as long as we cherish the moments we have together and support each other, we will be able to overcome any obstacles that come our way."

Love, laughter, and strength yet lay ahead down diverging paths, but the sacred sisterhood engraved upon their souls could never be obscured nor broken. Their tale, it seemed, had come full circle, two solitary souls woven eternally as one through compassion. Whatever wonders or hardships the future held, this enduring spiritual bond would light their way.

With a smile and a squeeze, Olivia whispered, "Our story is only beginning."

CHAPTER 15
A FUTURE OF PROMISE

The café was bustling as Olivia waited eagerly for Janice to arrive. It had been five years since they last saw each other in person, and Olivia was filled with excitement and nostalgia at the prospect of reconnecting with her dear friend. Soon, the door opened with the familiar chime, and Janice walked in, smiling brightly at Olivia.

"Livvy!" she exclaimed as they embraced warmly. After ordering their lunch, they found a seat by the window. "It is so good to see you," Olivia said. "I cannot believe it has been five years already!" Janice agreed, remarking how they both had changed yet their friendship endured.

Both girls, now 20 years old, had taken different paths. Olivia had the incredible opportunity to travel to a few different countries during her time away at school. She spent time in a rural village in Kenya, where she volunteered at a local school and helped with community development projects. Later, she traveled to India and worked with an organization that provided education and resources for children in impoverished areas. It was an eye-opening experience, witnessing the struggles that these communities faced and seeing the resilience and strength of the people there. Olivia learned so much from these experiences and felt truly humbled to be able to make a small impact on the lives of the underprivileged.

Janice, on the other hand, stayed in her hometown with her grandmother. She took some time to focus on her studies and continued to work part-time to help support her and her grandmother. She stayed involved with the local soup kitchen, which became an even bigger part of her life. It gave Janice a sense of purpose and allowed her to give back to the community.

Despite the physical distance between them, Janice and Olivia made sure to stay in contact. They would write letters to each other, sharing details about our lives and the challenges we faced. They also made it a point to have regular phone calls and video chats, catching up on everything that was going on and offering support in any way they could. It was not always easy, especially with their busy schedules and time zone differences, but their friendship was important to both, and they made the effort to stay connected. It was those moments of connection that helped Olivia and Janice navigate the ups and downs of life and keep their bond strong.

Seeing Janice after five long years of being apart was such a mix of emotions for Olivia. Excitement, nostalgia, and a sense of familiarity all flooded in as soon as she laid eyes on her. It was like a warm embrace for her soul, knowing that their friendship had endured despite the distance and time. There was a sense of comfort and connection that instantly came back as if they had never been apart. It was truly a heartwarming moment, one that reminded Olivia of the value and power of true friendship.

It was a mix of excitement, nervousness, and relief, all rolled into one for Janice as well. Seeing Olivia again brought back a flood of memories from their friendship, and she could not help but feel a sense of longing and anticipation to reconnect. However, there was a part of Janice that worried things might have changed, that maybe they would not be as close as they once were. But when she caught a glimpse of Olivia across the room, all those worries melted away. It was like no time had passed at all. The warmth in her smile and the familiar spark in her eyes reassured Janice that their bond was still strong.

At that moment, Janice felt a wave of gratitude for the deep connection they had built and the impact they had on each other's lives. Seeing Olivia again reminded Janice of the unwavering support they had always offered each other. It was a beautiful reminder that true friendship can withstand the test of time. Seeing Olivia after all those years it was like finding a missing puzzle piece and realizing that their friendship was meant to be a lasting one. It filled Janice with hope, excitement, and gratitude for the future they would continue to create together.

Janice shared her experiences in nursing school. She had always wanted to be a nurse, to help those in their time of need. Her dream was made possible, in part, thanks to Olivia's mom and dad. They had surprised Janice by offering to help with her nursing school tuition. After seeing how much she wanted to pursue her dreams of being a nurse, and to support her grandmother, they wanted to lend a helping hand. They also knew, despite their earlier reservations, that Janice truly was Olivia's best and dearest friend. It was incredibly generous of them, and Janice brought to tears, was never able to express how grateful she was for their support. They truly embody the spirit of friendship and kindness.

The Hanson family now considered Janice part of their family, just as Ruth considered Olivia part of her family. Janice was passionate about helping others and honoring her parents' memory through service.

Olivia told Janice about her studies in literature and aspirations to make a difference through storytelling. As they sat talking and laughing together, it felt like no time had passed at all. Their connection remained as strong as ever, rooted deeply in their journey, navigating life's challenges side by side.

Janice asked Olivia about her plans after college. Olivia revealed that she wanted to travel internationally and use storytelling as a tool to dismantle prejudices. Janice was inspired by Olivia's vision and promised to support her in any way. They reminisced on the winding path that brought them to this moment, filled with appreciation and hope for the roads ahead. Though they now walked separate paths, their bond would always be a guiding light.

Olivia smiled as Janice continued telling her about college. "That is amazing that you are doing so well working on your nursing degree," Olivia remarked. "You have always had such a caring spirit."

"I want to be able to provide medical care for underserved communities," Janice replied. "So many people slip through the cracks of the system. I think about all the times you supported me and my grandmother through difficult times. It made me realize how much of a difference a caring nurse can make."

Olivia nodded understandingly. "You are going to help so many people with your compassion. I always knew you were destined for great things." Janice grinned. "What can I say? You bring out the best in me. Our friendship has been such a blessing all these years. You inspire me to keep following my dreams and standing up for others."

As they reminisced on their journey so far, Olivia felt lucky to have such a selfless friend by her side. Janice's caring nature would surely heal many lives in her nursing career ahead. Olivia smiled, thinking of her experiences abroad. Knowing Olivia was enrolled in a work-study program overseas, she asked, "Tell me about some of your projects overseas," Janice asked eagerly.

"In Kenya, I volunteered with an organization empowering girls through education," Olivia began. "So many faced barriers but still showed incredible strength and resilience, just like you always have. They inspire me daily."

"That is amazing," Janice replied. "You have always had a gift for storytelling. I am sure you helped give those girls a voice."

Olivia nodded. "Your unwavering spirit in the face of adversity has stayed with me. I wanted to help break down prejudices like we faced. So, in South Africa, I interviewed women from different backgrounds and compiled their stories into an anthology."

"How powerful," Janice said. "Promoting understanding between all people is so important. You have come so far by applying the empathy and courage you learned from our friendship."

Olivia smiled. "I could not have done any of it without your guidance. You showed me the power we have when we lift each other up instead of tearing each other down."

Taking Janice's hand in hers, Olivia said sincerely, "Thank you for being my light in this world." Olivia squeezed Janice's hand, smiling warmly. "So much has changed since we first met," she said.

Janice nodded, gazing out the window contemplatively. "I still remember spilling hot chocolate all over you like it was yesterday," she chuckled. "Who knew that chance encounter would lead us here."

"You gave me so much strength during the hardest times," Olivia replied. "All those cruel words and judgments we faced, yet our bond never faltered. We taught each other what it truly means to have empathy, courage, and resilience."

"You are, and will always be, my best friend," Janice said softly, meeting Olivia's eyes. "We have been through so much together, and you have always loved and accepted me unconditionally. I am the luckiest person because of that."

Olivia shook her head. "I am the lucky one. Our friendship has opened my eyes to the realities others face and how I can help others and lift them up. You inspire me daily to keep growing."

Glancing at each other with affection, they fell into a contented silence, nibbling at their food, grateful for the profound lessons and joy their chance meeting had brought forth.

Just then, a familiar voice called out. "Well, if it is not my two favorite girls!" Olivia and Janice turned with delighted smiles to see Ruth, Janice's grandmother, making her way over. Ruth enveloped them both in a hug, then slid into the booth next to Janice, "It is so wonderful to see you both," she said. "You have come such a long way since you first met. I am glad your friendship has endured, especially after facing those closed-minded folks all those years ago."

It has been a few tough years since Ruth's heart attack, but she has been doing well. After the incident, she received the medical care she needed and went through a period of recovery and rehabilitation. It took some time for her to regain her strength and adjust to some lifestyle changes, but she has shown incredible resilience and determination. She has also been taking better care of herself (Janice sees to this), following her doctor's advice, and making healthier choices. It brings Janice so much joy to see her smiling, active, and enjoying life again.

Ruth will still have to be cautious and mindful of her health, but overall, her progress has been remarkable. She remains a strong woman, and Janice is grateful every day for her presence and the love and support she continues to provide.

"We could not have done it without your support, grandmother," Janice replied affectionately. "And Olivia's been like family to us."

Ruth nodded knowingly. "I could see from the beginning the bond you two shared. It warms my heart to see how you have stood by each other through every obstacle. Your care and understanding set an example for the rest of the world."

Olivia took Ruth's hand in hers. "We are forever grateful to you for everything you have done as well. Your guidance helped shape us into who we are."

Ruth smiled, eyes glistening. "I am proud to call you both my girls. Now come, tell me more about your travels and studies!" They spent the afternoon reconnecting as a family, cherishing their unbreakable bonds.

Olivia smiled shyly at Janice. "I actually have something to show you." She produced a book from her bag. Janice gasped when she read the title, 'The Beauty of Unlikely Friendships.'

"I wanted to publish our story," Olivia said. "To share the message of hope, courage, and empathy we learned. Your guidance helped me overcome so much, and I hope it can inspire others facing adversity, too."

Janice flipped through the pages, tears brimming. She paused at a photo of them as teens, beaming happily together. It was like reliving those memories all over again.

"Olivia, this is breathtaking," Janice said in wonder. "Our story will truly touch so many hearts. You found such beauty and strength even in our darkest times. I am incredibly honored you decided to share it."

Olivia took Janice's hands. "None of it would have been possible without you. Your kindness and spirit of resilience taught me to keep walking forward, even when faced with cruelty. Our bond has only grown brighter over the years."

Janice embraced her friend, fully appreciating what they had overcome to reach this point. Looking toward a future of growth and understanding, their story remains an unlikely friendship that continues to blossom anew each day.

"Olivia," Janice said pensively, "this book will do so much good."

"I am getting messages from readers who feel inspired by our story," Olivia replied. "How we overcame bullying and prejudice through compassion. It has given them the courage to stand up to their own hardships."

Janice smiled softly. "All those years ago, I never imagined the impact our friendship would have. We were just two girls supporting each other against the odds."

"That is what makes our story so powerful," said Olivia. "When people lift each other up with empathy and understanding instead of tearing each other down, real change can happen. You taught me that."

"I will always be grateful for the strength and wisdom you brought to my life," Janice replied, taking Olivia's hand affectionately. "If telling our journey helps even one person, it is worth it."

Olivia nodded. "Your love has guided me since the first day we met. Sharing this story with the world is my way of honoring the profound gift of our unlikely bond and all you have given to me."

Gazing at each other with pride and gratitude, Olivia and Janice marveled at how far their story had come and all the lives it would continue to touch. They then realized Olivia's return flight was approaching and had to get to the airport. As they got up to leave, Olivia and Ruth hugged each other warmly, tears in each other's eyes.

"I am going to miss you so much," Ruth said.

Olivia, shaking with sadness, replied, "And I will miss you as well. I cannot express the love and gratitude I have for you allowing me to be part of your family."

Olivia's father drove them to the airport. The drive was bittersweet. As the two girls sat in the car together, the atmosphere was a mix of excitement and sadness. There was a certain heaviness in knowing that they would be separated again, but also a sense of hope for what the future held for both. They talked about their plans, dreams, and all the memories they had created together; all the while, Olivia's dad smiled in silence. There were moments of laughter, reminiscing about the adventures they had shared and the lessons they had learned from each other. But underneath it all, there was a deep sense of gratitude and a profound appreciation for the bond they had rekindled. The realization that this friendship had stood the test of time and come out stronger on the other side was both humbling and incredibly empowering.

They held each other's hands, cherishing the closeness they had regained after years apart. The drive was filled with both silence and meaningful conversations as they soaked in their last moments together before reaching the airport.

Olivia turned to Janice at the airport gate, eyes glistening. "I cannot believe this visit is over already", Olivia said, embracing her dear friend tightly. "But I know our love and friendship will last forever, no matter how far apart we are."

"You will always have a home with me," Janice replied. "And I will be waiting here whenever you are ready to come back." They walked to the window, watching planes take off underneath the setting sun. So much had changed since they first met, yet their connection remained unwavering.

Saying goodbye to Olivia at the airport was one of the most sentimental moments of Janice's life. Waves of emotions washed over her, and it was hard to put into words exactly how she felt. There was a deep sense of sadness, knowing they would be physically apart once again, but also a profound gratitude for the time they had spent together.

As they stood there, hugging tightly, tears welled up in her eyes. It was tough to say goodbye, knowing that life would take them on different paths. They had grown so much together, supporting and inspiring each other, and the thought of not having her physically by her side was heartbreaking to Janice. But amid the sadness, there was also a sense of pride. Seeing how far they had come and how much they had grown as individuals gave her a sense of fulfillment. Their friendship, Janice knew, had impacted their lives in ways that she could never have imagined, and that realization filled her heart with a mix of joy and gratitude.

In that moment at the airport, as they embraced for the last time before parting ways, Olivia was overwhelmed by a mixture of sadness, gratitude, and a deep sense of appreciation for the bond they had shared. It was a reminder that even though distance may separate them, the memories and lessons they had gained from their friendship would forever remain with them.

"All these years later and, you are still my greatest teacher," Olivia said, squeezing Janice's hand. "Thank you for being my light."

Janice smiled through happy tears. "And thank you for being mine. Our story is just beginning; I cannot wait to see all the lives we will continue touching together."

Before they parted ways with the promise of reuniting again soon, Olivia felt gratitude for the profound lessons of courage, empathy, and strength that Janice had imparted. Their friendship continued to blossom anew each day, roots grounded deeply in understanding and acceptance.

With one final hug and wave, Olivia boarded her flight, heart filled with eternal joy and understanding their unlikely friendship had brought. Wherever the future led, this bond would endure forever as their greatest blessing.

Janice and Olivia's father walked towards the car, arms around each other. Janice knew he was not her father, but it sure did feel like he was.

Arriving home, thinking she had no more tears to shed, she retrieved the mail from her mailbox. There was a handwritten envelope addressed to her, the handwriting unfamiliar. As she read the letter, tears welled up in her eyes.

Dear Janice,

My name is Sophia. Last year, during hard times, I found comfort in your story. My brother was facing prejudice and ridicule, and I did not know how to help. Your message of empathy I read about in the book written by Olivia Hanson, inspired me. I organized a student group promoting inclusion. It brought our divided community together and provided hope to those facing cruelty. Your courage alongside Olivia reminds us that understanding can overcome any divide.

Today, my brother is thriving thanks to support from friends like you. I wanted to thank you for sharing your journey, it changed my life and so many others. You proved that even the unlikeliest bonds have the power to uplift the world.

Wishing you continued strength. Remember that through trials, compassion will guide our way.

With Gratitude,

Sophia

Janice smiled through her tears, filled with pride. One small act of kindness had touched so many. She could not wait to share the letter with Olivia and her grandmother, grateful their story continued empowering souls everywhere. Their message of hope would endure for generations to come. Janice held the heartfelt letter close, reflecting on their incredible journey.

So much had changed since that fateful Sunday when she first met Olivia. Through empathy, courage, and compassion, their unlikely bond became a lifelong sisterhood guiding each other. Now, their story touched communities globally, empowering those facing cruelty to overcome divisions through understanding. Sophia's words proved even darkness cannot extinguish hope's eternal flame. Janice thought of Olivia, proud of their journey teaching acceptance. Though challenges would come, standing united in love meant prevailing over any storm. Their message endures that wisdom emerges through embracing differences with care.

Small acts borne of empathy truly do make all the difference, helping lost souls find their light again. And Janice knew, that wherever life led, her and Olivia's bond of sisterhood would forever be humanity's greatest teacher. With gratitude for lessons learned and lives yet to be inspired, Janice gazed proudly at the sunset, certain their story of rekindled faith would endure through generations as a beacon of hope for all who face adversity alone no more.

Janice rubbed the friendship bracelet she still wore and went to show her grandmother the letter she had received.

Printed in the USA
CPSIA information can be obtained
at www.ICGtesting.com
LVHW091807250724
786322LV00001B/96